I Was Amelia Earhart

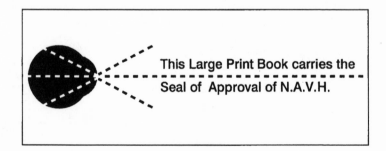

This Large Print Book carries the
Seal of Approval of N.A.V.H.

I Was Amelia Earhart

Jane Mendelsohn

Thorndike Press • Thorndike, Maine

Published in 1996 by arrangement with Alfred A. Knopf, Inc.

Thorndike Large Print ® Americana Series.

The tree indicium is a trademark of Thorndike Press.

The text of this Large Print edition is unabridged.
Other aspects of the book may vary from the original edition.

Set in 16 pt. Bookman Old Style.

Printed in the Unites States on permanent paper.

Library of Congress Cataloging in Publication Data

Mendelsohn, Jane, 1965–
    I was Amelia Earhart : a novel / Jane Mendelsohn.
      p.   cm.
    ISBN 0-7862-0858-9 (lg. print : hc)
    ISBN 0-7862-0859-7 (lg. print : sc)
    1. Earhart, Amelia, 1897–1937 — Fiction. 2. Large type
books. I. Title.
    [PS3563.E482I2 1996b]
    813′.54—dc20   96-27420

For Nick

But in the roar of the wind she heard the roar of an aeroplane coming nearer and nearer.
— VIRGINIA WOOLF, *Orlando*

The sky is flesh.

The great blue belly arches up above the water and bends down behind the line of the horizon. It's a sight that has exhausted its magnificence for me over the years, but now I seem to be seeing it for the first time.

More and more now, I remember things. Images, my life, the sky. Sometimes I remember the life I used to live, and it feels impossibly far away. It's always there, a part of me, in the back of my mind, but it doesn't seem real. Whether life is more real than death, I don't know. What I know is that the life I've lived since I died feels more real to me than the one I lived before.

I know this: I risked my life without living it. Noonan once said any fool could have seen I was risking my life but not living it. I had already been flying for a long time when he said that. It was 1937. I was thirty-nine. I was more beautiful than ever, but an aura of unhappiness traveled with me, like the trail of a falling comet. I felt as though I had already lived my entire life, having flown the Atlantic and set several world records, and there was no one to share my sadness with, least of all my husband. Charmed by my style and my daring exploits, the public continued to send me flowers and gifts, but the love of strangers meant nothing to me. My luminous existence left me longing and bored. I had no idea what it meant to live an entire life. I was still very young.

So, the sky.

It's the only sky that I can remember, the only one that speaks to me now.

I'm flying around the world, there's nothing but sky. The sky is flesh. It's the last sky.

I remember: I'm flying around the world. I'm flying over the Pacific somewhere off the coast of New Guinea in my twin-engine Lockheed Electra, and I'm lost. I watch the sky as it curves and swells, and every now and then I think I can see it shudder. Voluptuous, sultry in the naked heat, it seems to me to be the flesh of a woman. But then suddenly the light illuminates a stretch of more masculine proportions — a muscular passage of azure heft, a wide plank like the back of a hand — and I have to acknowledge, although I hate to admit it, the bisexuality of nature. I purse my lips a little when I realize this, and scrunch my nose up to rearrange my goggles. My eyes and my eyes reflected in the windshield hold the sun in them, and it burns. I blink and reach one arm directly overhead. My fingers grasp a dial. Out of the far corner of my field of vision, I catch a glimpse of the underlying sea. Thinking to myself that this might be the last day of my life, that I'm hot, and that I am hungry, I adjust the dial and lower my arm. The sea is dark. It is darker than the sky.

This is the story of what happened to me when I died. It's also the story of my life. Destiny, the alchemy of fate and luck. I think about it sometimes, under a radiant sun. The tide laughs. The light swims. I watch the fish-skeleton shadows of the palm leaves on the sand. The clouds ripped to shreds.

Today when I think of my former life, I think of it as a dream. In the dream I am another person. In the dream I am the most famous aviatrix of my day, a heroine. I am Amelia Earhart.

Part One

One

As far back as she could remember, she always wanted to be a heroine. She settled on her vocation in the nickelodeon, where bathed in the mechanical shadows of earthly stars, she fell under the spell of Cleopatra and Joan of Arc, their silent swoons and voiceless battle cries calling her off to distant lands. Even before she understood what a heroine was, she knew that she wanted to be one. Not on a screen in a dusty old vaudeville house, but out in the real world. The painted goddesses ruling countries and fighting wars weren't at all like the women she knew. The women she knew did what men expected of them. Heroines, they did whatever they wanted. They smoked cigarettes on horseback under silken skies. They carried guns and had a multitude of lovers. She was seduced by the vision of an imaginary world

13

where women led extraordinary lives, and when the picture was about factory workers or men kissing their secretaries, she snuck behind the stage and played checkers or penny poker with the manager's one-handed son.

Sometimes my thoughts are clearly mine, I hear them speak to me, in my own voice. Other times I see myself from far away, and my thoughts are ghostly, aerial, in the third person.

When I was very young, six or seven, I already wanted to die. I already had the dream. I wanted to escape, to go higher, to leave my body, and this made me seem ambitious, greedy for life. When I was young, people hated my greediness, but they enjoyed it too. A little girl filled with desire is a beautiful sight, ugly, but very beautiful.

My father gave me a gun for Christmas, against my grandfather's wishes. It was a .22 caliber rifle. I used to hunt for rats in my grandparents' barn, the milky winter light falling down between the rafters, scraps of hay dust floating like lazy planets. I'd lift my rifle slowly, like a cowboy on the plains, and press my eyelashes up against the barrel. When you shoot a rat, it falls over in a soft heap. I liked the look of a dead rat, so peaceful.

The sky is flesh. I'm flying around the world. A fine perspiration laces my face and neck. It begins to seep down my back. Twisting my left arm around behind me, I locate a can on a shelf. I grab hold of the screwdriver and steadying the can in my lap, I poke two holes through its metal skin. When I poke the holes, I hear a tiny pop, like the release of a toy gun. Inside the plane, the mindless roar of the engine plays a dull accompaniment to my snack. When I finish the juice, I put the can back on the shelf and lick the last drops of salt from my lips.

This is what's happening: I'm flying over the Pacific somewhere off the coast of New Guinea in my twin-engine Lockheed Electra, and I'm lost. This is my predicament. I fiddle with the radio the way I have fiddled with it so many times before, only this time I receive nothing. I look down at my fuel gauge and my eyeballs tremble rapidly as they follow the small, significant movements of the indicator. My radio is useless, I'm running out of gas, and I'm suffering from dehydration and fatigue.

I wish I had a piece of chocolate, I say, out loud, above the roar of the engine.

Clouds gather beneath me. Gauzy, insubstantial ribbons of cloud veiling the green sea. Then endless stretches of extreme whiteness uninterrupted by sea. I travel through valleys of unformulated cloud dissolving and recovering itself. After a while it begins to take shape again, weightier hills of lather rolling down to nowhere, breaking up into islands of pinkish white, separated by sudden shocks of blue.

I like to lose myself in the beauty of the sky, but today I seem unable to fall in love with my surroundings without being yanked back to the gravity of my predicament. I'm a practical escapist, and every movement of my mind, each digression from dream to reality and back again, is a faithful expression of my character.

Weaving in and out of the strange clouds, hidden in my tiny cockpit, submerged, alone, on the magnitude of this weird, unhuman space, I feel as if I'm not alive. That's what I want, that feeling. I want this dream of death I'm passing through.

Once, when I was a little girl, my father took me for a ride on a roller coaster. The day was breezy and crowded, with lots of starched puffy clouds in the sky. We were at a fairgrounds, and as I waited in line I heard a band playing off in the distance. When my turn finally came, I allowed my father to help me into the wooden car. I felt the touch of his large hand and the dryness of his wide taut palm. I allowed him to lift me into the rickety seat. After strapping me onto the bench, he climbed in next to me. Well, he sighed, this is going to be fun. He showed me how to clasp my hand around the safety bar, letting me know with a gentle but nervous smile that if I needed to, I could hold on to his arm. By then the four double seats behind us had been filled, and the operator was cranking up the machinery. As the ground beneath me started to move, I recognized that I was experiencing sensations I had never felt before. Making our way up the narrow track, I watched the spectators down below me grow smaller and smaller. It was a strange state: I couldn't tell which was moving, myself or the world. But when the ride picked up speed and I could feel the wind against my face — I saw my mother and my sister in a blur of light, balanced on a strand of my hair — I knew it was myself and not the world that moved, and this cataclysm of perspective changed my life.

I always hated wearing goggles. But I wear them when I have to, and that day, the last day, the day the sky is flesh, I'm wearing goggles, and a leather skullcap, and a scarf around my neck. I put on the goggles only when absolutely necessary, and I never put them on before I get into the cockpit and I take them off before I climb out of the hatch. Ever since I've been famous, which has been a long time now, I've taken great care with my personal style. I wear my hair short, I like it that way, and I smile with my lips closed, the way G.P. taught me. After I flew across the Atlantic and became famous, G.P. decided to mold me into a star. He told me how to eat, how to speak, how to dress, how to smile, with my mouth closed, for the cameras. He told me not to wear hats with feathers or brims, but I ignored him whenever I could.

On the plane that day, I'm wearing my typical uniform of brown leather pants and a white silk shirt. I've been flying for weeks, with only a change of clothes, but still I look fashionable. No one wore leather and silk with as much glamorous nonchalance. The look is my own, I invented it for myself long before I met G.P., when I was first learning how to fly. I wanted the other pilots to take me seriously, but I was a society girl. A fallen socialite, from unexceptional circumstances, but still they were skeptical of me, and I wanted desperately to impress them. This was the time in my life when I cut my long, golden hair until it was short and then I curled it. It was also the time when I bought a leather coat, to fit in with the crowd at the airfield. I slept in it the first night I bought it, because I loved it and because I wanted to break it in. Then I splattered it with oil, on purpose, to make stains.

In the cockpit, next to my head, hangs a bamboo fishing pole which reaches back into the navigator's cabin. It's a makeshift telephone, used to pass messages back and forth between pilot and navigator. We installed it in Miami and it served us well, back in the days when we were communicating. Now it shivers gently in time with the plane's fluctuations, and points like a shaky, accusing finger toward the rear cabin.

Back then, a plane was called a ship. There were still cabins, and a sense of voyaging. There was a reverence for flight because it was so dangerous. People lost themselves. There was no safety.

Inside the cabin there's a man passed out with his face on an open map. His head lies in the Pacific like a dark eighth continent, and his long arms wrap around the ocean as if he were a sweetly uncoordinated god trying to scoop it up. His blue-black hair swings forward over his face, strands of it sticking to his forehead and neck. After a month on the road, he needs a haircut. His grease-stained coveralls, pulled taut over his bent knees, reach only as far as his midcalf, revealing underneath the navigator's illuminated table his coarse, curly leg hair, his dark-blue socks, and the untied shoelace on his brown left shoe. Next to his right foot lies an empty bottle, a last swill of coppery liquid puddled inside. Every now and then he kicks it in his sleep and sends the glass rolling away and then back again. As it rolls, the puddle of liquor remains miraculously still.

He is a former Pan American Airlines navigator, a master mariner unlimited, and a certified first-class Mississippi riverboat captain. We are not lovers. We have never been lovers. We could not have been further from being lovers unless we had never met. Neither one of us finds the other attractive. We are handsome and beautiful in timeless ways — I with my boyish grace and open expression, he with his deep eyes and slow smile. But to me, the navigator is the least manly of men. He is persnickety, easily frightened, and irresponsible. To him I embody the most unfeminine qualities: I am dogmatic, demanding, and impolite. I am impatient and unkind when frustrated. I swear. And I have not one self-sacrificing, maternal bone in my unwomanly, muscular body.

I've had lovers. I've had a husband. My husband proposed to me six times before I would accept. And then, when I finally did accept, I wrote him a letter asking him to promise to let me go. Let me go in a year if I'm unhappy, I said. It sounded so grave, but I was only being practical. The idea that we would be bound together irrevocably seemed ridiculous. But I was not in love.

I remember the first time I met my husband: I couldn't stand him. He was arrogant. He held the door open for me with his whole arm.

He was interviewing me for a job. The job was to be the first woman to fly across the Atlantic. The plane was going to be flown by a man, but they wanted a woman to sit in the plane, to make the record, for publicity purposes. They wanted me as baggage. I knew I could fly the plane myself, but I had to accept their terms. I wasn't going to have a career as a pilot any other way. I wasn't rich. Most of the other women flying planes were wealthy.

As my future husband pointed out to me, if I went, and if the flight was successful, there would be other opportunities. He glanced at his gold watch. He was a man who understood opportunity. Sometimes it seemed as if he had invented the very idea.

He was right, of course. Later, I flew the Atlantic myself. Then the Pacific. But the first time, I just went along for the ride.

He was the son of a wealthy publishing family. He was used to having his way, with men and women. He had a kind of studied New York charm, which I hated. If I had to say what it was about him that made me marry him, I would say that it was his persistence, not his charm. I admired his determination, but his was a transparent, demanding, foolish charm. He had a way of monopolizing attention that made him appear desperate, more so than he really was.

But I can't complain, really. Sometimes he did it for me.

Only much later did I realize what I had done by marrying him. I didn't blame myself, but I realized that I had surrendered to the whims of men — even I who had been so bold and independent, even I who had taken on the humiliating task of sitting in the back of an airplane like cargo when I knew perfectly well that I could fly it myself better than the so-called pilot in the cockpit — I realized that I had surrendered so easily because I had been, despite my most vigilant efforts, infatuated with the men who made the rules. Sitting in my future husband's office, listening to the drone of his comfortable voice, I felt an infinite rush of sympathy for him. I knew he was hidden, even from himself, and I wanted to be the only person who really knew him. Later, this realization made me suspect that I had loved my husband. Selfishly, but at least I had loved him.

His name was George Palmer Putnam. He helped me into a taxi after the interview, his umbrella shielding me but not himself from the rain, a drop of water hanging gallantly off his nose. Then I drove off to the train station, through the park at the gentlest point of dusk.

Two

By 1937, at the tender age of thirty-nine, she was the loneliest of heroines. She was more expressive around the eyes, and no movie star seemed as mysterious as she or wore leather and silk with such glamorous nonchalance. But she felt as though she had already lived her entire life, having crossed the Atlantic solo and set several world records, and she had no one to share her sadness with, least of all her husband. Her husband, G.P., her business manager. He's the husband who made her famous, who devoted himself to her, even when she hated him, even when he hated her back. She needs him so that she can fly, so that she can escape from him, so that she can escape from the very people who worship her.

Thirty-nine. I have been famous for a long time, and I am still dependent, on the world, on G.P., on my unhappiness. But I want to fly. I want to fly around the world. The flight around the world contains within it everything inside me, all the life and all the death. I want to take the life and the death that is inside me and make something of it. But I'm tired, and careless now. And my husband, who wants me to do it for the money, doesn't see that my carelessness will kill me. Or maybe he does. I leave the details up to him. I want my dream, but I am so tired. I tell him I want to go alone, that I don't want a navigator, but he insists on it and we argue. I tell him that instead we should put a signal on Howland Island, that I won't find it without a signal. He ignores me when I say this. He keeps eating. He places his knife on the side of his plate and he keeps chewing.

The great heroine is preparing to land. She's coming into the airfield, bracing herself with the usual aplomb. Her ship makes its way through a furrowed landscape of white, and for several minutes visibility is completely obscured. Then she sees him. On the dusty tarmac surrounded by flat gray hangars, a man in a hat stands waiting for her. His tie lifting, lifting higher as she lets down her wheels. He takes off his hat when the wind picks up, as if he were taking it off for a funeral. Pulling his pant leg up before he bends his knee, he climbs onto the wing when she stops the plane and reaches his hand out to her when she emerges.

The Miami *Herald* is here, he says.

Hello, G.P., she says.

She pulls herself out of the hatch and stands on the wing. She loosens her silk scarf. On the tarmac three men in summer-weight suits and pale fedoras are walking toward her.

That was some landing, one of them says.

Did you think you were going to have a crack-up?

I certainly smacked it down hard that time. She climbs down from the wing.

Is it true that you're planning an around-the-world flight?

I've tried that already, haven't I?

Yes, but we heard you were planning another.

The best-laid plans, gentlemen.

On the ground she is holding her husband's hand. He nods to the reporters, who step aside. A photographer crouches to take a picture. It is still early morning but the sun is blinding. They pose for a moment and then walk on.

Although secretly she fears that she is getting old, which she is for a woman pilot, she continues to plan death-defying journeys. But she compensates for her increasingly disturbing lack of optimism by projecting an image of unflappable calm. She is not only America's most beloved female flyer, she is also its most brilliant undiscovered actress. Still, and this bothers her although she pretends that it doesn't, her shameless love of danger and the cavalier way she has relinquished her so-called feminine duties have won her slightly less respect and affection than she deserves.

That night we have dinner at the hotel. It's one of the new hotels along the water, low and pink, with ocean-liner curves. The radio plays a song called "Harbor Lights," and the Four Cadets are singing. I'm very tired and eat with my head down. G.P. is talking to the airport manager who has driven us to the hotel. During the meal I say something about putting a signal on Howland Island, and G.P. ignores my remark. He keeps eating. I stop eating and stare at my plate and when I don't look up he lowers his fork. The airport manager licks the sauce from his spoon. Then G.P. pulls on his cuff as if it will prove something and says, If we put a signal on Howland Island, the book won't sell out by Christmas.

He makes me write. He makes me write for magazines and columns in newspapers and he makes me write books about my flights. I wrote earnest poetry in high school, but he isn't interested in my poems. He doesn't realize how difficult it is to write. Later, Noonan will read one of my books. He will say to me, As a writer, you're a good pilot. But G.P. is smart and the books sell very well and the money enables me to fly.

Upstairs I sit outside on a small terrace that is painted candy-colored pink. A breeze blows over from the ocean. I slip off my shoes and feel the painted cement smooth and grainy underfoot. I ride my mind on the waves for a while, just listening to their murmur.

Later, I put on a dressing gown and sit up in bed, reading maps. When G.P. comes in I am studying a chart of weather conditions over Africa.

What was that all about? he says, removing his jacket and loosening his tie.

I'm very tired.

You should be asleep.

I'm too tired to sleep.

He walks out onto the terrace and lights a cigarette. When he's done he walks in and pulls the drapes. In his unbuttoned shirt and his white cotton shorts he sits down on the edge of the bed.

It's too late to change the radio, he says. And it's too late to put a signal on Howland Island. But if you feel that it's absolutely necessary . . .

I don't feel that about anything anymore.

Do you still want to go?

Of course I want to. I'm going. But not because it's necessary.

The sky is flesh.

This is the sentence that I will use to begin my book about the flight.

When she opens her mouth, a monstrous scream.

She leans down toward the microphone and repeats herself.

She says, On June first, nineteen thirty-seven, I will depart from Miami on my second attempt to fly around the world. I will be traveling along an equatorial route. I will be flying my trusty Lockheed Electra. And I will be flying with my navigator, Mr. Fred Noonan.

Thank you, Miss Earhart. Sorry about the technical difficulty.

That's quite all right.

Miss Earhart, would you like to tell our radio listeners anything else about your upcoming trip?

I'm very much looking forward to it.

What I think the public would most like to know, Miss Earhart, is why, why do such a daredevil kind of thing?

Because I want to. And because I think women should do for themselves the things that men have done, and have not done.

Thank you, Miss Earhart. And good luck to you. The American people will be cheering for you and praying for you on June first.

A high-pitched hum sounds when he turns off the microphone. A young woman wearing a cardigan and carrying a clipboard speaks from the other side of a glass wall.

Miss Earhart, your husband is here to take you to the airport.

Thank you. Where is the ladies' room?

Through this door and down that hall.

Thank you. I'll be right back.

She's had a headache all morning. G.P. says it's her teeth. He's scheduled a dentist appointment for this afternoon, although she's told him that it won't do any good. Turning the round metal knob on the heavy door, she steps into a pale and stuffy room. Inside there are two stalls and two sinks and one shell-shaped sconce on either side of the mirror. The lights are off. A diffuse beam of daylight filters down from a frosted window. Under the window sits a low pillowed chair. Beside it, a standing ashtray.

In the mirror above the sink she sees the circles under her eyes. She runs her fingers through her short, sandy hair. She's wearing a dress because there will be reporters outside the radio station, many of them, and she adjusts the neckline, which has fallen over to the left. She turns from the mirror, opens her purse, removes a silver powder compact and powders her face. She sees her reflection in the larger mirror, powdering her face.

My first crack-up was with my flying teacher, Neta, in a plane called the Canary. As we approached a grove of eucalyptus, the engine stalled and we tore into the trees. We smashed the undercarriage and the propeller. I remember crawling out of the mess, my coveralls torn and my brain intoxicated with the heady, mentholated smell of eucalyptus. By the time Neta turned around to look for me, I had fished out my silver compact and was powdering my nose.

When she asked me as a joke if I was meeting someone there, I answered her with the charming, deadpan etiquette for which I would become famous.

I might as well look fresh when the reporters get here, I said.

* * *

I tilt the compact to view myself from the side: a printed dress falling in silky folds, pale stockings the color of buttermilk, low-heeled lace-up calfskin shoes pointing slightly inward.

I close the compact and turn toward the mirror. I stare at my face for a while. I have the same expression I've always had, the small nose, the wide eyes, the grin. But I notice a pucker of worry over my brow, a network of lines around my eyes. Behind me in the mirror I glimpse the chair and the ashtray. I remember a department store in Atchison, Kansas, where my grandmother used to shop. A brightly floral ladies' lounge on the top floor of the building, with a picture window overlooking the street. Marble sinks and a blue chaise longue upholstered in damask silk. A heavy smell of perfume and disinfectant. I remember winter afternoons, shopping for Christmas clothes, escaping to the ladies' room and staring out the window. The purple sky lowering its velvety curtain. My face afloat in the glass. Eerie and disembodied, it took shape in the darkness with a languid speed, decorated by the lights of the windows

36

across the street, and beyond that . . .

Miss Earhart, is everything all right in there?

Oh, yes. I'm fine. Thank you.

Your husband asked me to remind you that he's waiting outside.

I'll be right there.

. . . the early stars.

When she emerges from behind a swinging glass door, the shadows of the station's letters fly briefly like hidden feelings across her face.

The sun is low and the plane is hot. Its wings cast gigantic shadows. Later, a reporter arrives to talk with her. Owen, he's an old friend by now, he's covered her flights for so long. Sometimes she thinks he's her only friend. The two of them walk on the runway for a while, their long shadows circling as they change direction, the light in their hair reddish and gold. She is wearing white coveralls, splattered with oil. He's wearing a suit and a hat.

When she squints into the distance, he stares at her. Anyone can see that he's in love.

How does that thing feel? He points

to her mouth.

Awful, she says. It's giving me a head-ache.

I think a good radio and a sober navigator would take care of the head-aches.

Owen, you think too much. Have you seen Noonan?

No, not yet. I hear he smashed up his car again, with what's-her-name in it, the second wife.

It's terrible but sort of funny, isn't it?

I don't think so. Why are you taking him?

She leans down and picks a bottle cap off the ground. G.P. insists, she says.

You want to go alone.

She flicks the cap into the weeds. I can't always do what I want.

He loosens his tie and takes it off. He rolls it up and stuffs it in his pocket.

Fred's a good navigator, she says.

He's a drunk.

She nods.

So why the charity?

Old age, I suppose.

Old what?

Age. I have a morbid obsession with it.

I guess even Amelia Earhart has to be

afraid of something.

Well, she says. Don't print it.

A warm wind picks up and blows his hat off. They both run after it in the dusty light.

Amelia?

Yes.

Nothing.

All right. I'll ask you something then.

Anything.

You have to be honest.

He crosses his heart.

What do you think are my chances?

Your chances of finding Howland Island?

He stops. He puts his hands in his pockets. It's a small island, he says.

Smaller than the Cleveland airport.

It's in the middle of the ocean.

I know.

He takes a moment.

Fifty-fifty, he says. Being optimistic.

The sun has just fallen above the hangars, where it sits in a pool of blood. When he looks at her, she's looking at something he can't see. He says he hopes that she's being careful.

Fifty-fifty, she says, smiling past him, past the sunset. I think I can live with that.

I had to take Noonan with me because we had run out of money and he was the cheapest navigator we could find. G.P. said he was the best, and that may have been true, but he was definitely the cheapest. He was cheap because he'd been fired from Pan Am for drinking and he couldn't find another job. I didn't want to take him. I didn't want to take anybody. I wanted to be alone.

It's two days before the flight, and she's driving to the airfield. G.P. reads telegrams to her while he drives. Best of luck. Best wishes. Your courage is an inspiration. We applaud you. We salute you. We admire you.

Where is the one from Eleanor and the President?

I read it to you.

Read it to me again.

He reads it again and they both smile.

That's awfully nice of them, isn't it? She has the window rolled down, and bursts of breeze blow in. Her sleeve ripples in the wind.

It's going to be hot today.

It's a scorcher.

They pass streets lined with palms

and Spanish-style houses, a strip of stores with handwritten signs. Then groves of oranges, rows of squat trees, the leaves dark and thick on the branches. By the side of the road, a man sells fruit out of a crate. A family showers under a hose. A buzzing in the air from the electrical wires. Black birds line the wires, like stubble.

She looks over at him and nods her head.

Hey, she flirts, read it again.

When we get to the airstrip I pull the car up onto the field and stride over to my plane with my hands in my pockets. I'm already wearing my coveralls and I'm smiling, scrunching my nose up and squinting against the sun. Several mechanics are talking in the shade of the hangar; some sit on fuel drums, some are standing. I head over to them and they say hello and some kick the ground and put out their cigarettes. We walk over to the plane and begin working. We work on the fuel gauge and fix a wire on the engine. We patch up the leaking oil lines. Overhead, early traces of cloud have blown away and the sky is a brilliant mirror. Two technicians fiddle with the radio and ask me if it's true that I only use it to listen to music. They joke with me about this and I laugh and say it's true and at around twelve noon a beat-up Ford pulls up and a man gets out and we stop joking. He wears a dark double-breasted suit and polished shoes and he's carrying a paper bag. A white handkerchief peeps out of his breast pocket. His white shirt is starched and cleanly pressed and he is not wearing a hat. He wears his hair lightly slicked, and it shines like leather in the sun. He's tall and his stride is long and athletic, although he isn't in a hurry. As he approaches the plane he is smiling and very handsome and he glances around. Then he looks at me.

When I saw Noonan, he was the last person in the world I wanted to see.

I look at the paper bag and then look at him. What a surprise. We weren't expecting you until tomorrow.

He says he couldn't stay away. He says hello to the mechanics. How does she look? he says, looking at me.

I climb down from the plane and hold out my hand.

She's looking fine. We're working on the radio.

I have grease on my face and a screw-driver in my hand. He knows that I don't like him.

He plants a kiss on my cheek and I smile wanly.

What's in the bag, I ask, looking him straight in the eye.

A pint. He gives me a confessional expression. Oh, don't look so sad, Captain. I'm only kidding. Come back here, I'm only joking.

He hands me the bag and I open it up. I pull out two pairs of eyeglasses.

Spectacles, Mr. Noonan?

I told you I was joking.

That's what I need, a blind navigator.

I drop the bag on the ground and walk away. He bends down and picks up his glasses gently. Don't do that, he says. Really, you shouldn't have done that. I just bought these, they weren't cheap.

I thought you already had a pair of glasses.

I sat on them on the way here.

You sat on them.

He looks up at me and lets his arms hang down in a position of supplicant helplessness.

You sat on them, this time exasper-ated but yielding. What the hell am I going to do with you?

He blows the dust off his glasses and brushes the dust off the front of his pants. He takes the handkerchief out of his pocket and wipes his face and neck and then he folds the handkerchief again and puts it back in his pocket. He looks at her, looks into her eyes.

Then he says: Take me around the world.

That night she and G.P. are invited to a party at the home of a Miami businessman. On the way there, G.P. says something about Noonan just showing up like that and she asks him to open his window. The night is warm and fruity, and as they turn onto a narrow road a salty ocean smell engulfs them and recedes. The trees along the side of the road give way to tall dry bushes and low willowy weeds. The low late sun is caught in the mirror. The sky spreads pink and yellow and orange.

You know I've never wanted to take him, she says.

But he's the best, I thought we agreed on that.

44

Then why did you have to bring it up?

Perhaps I'm nervous. I *am* your husband.

Oh, is that what you are.

He shuts his window and looks down and pulls on his cuff. I want to talk to you about the *Herald Tribune.* They're expecting a letter from each location, which, as you know, we'll use for the book. And I've arranged for three calls. The first one from Karachi. We'll have them recorded. And I'm working on getting us a broadcast from Honolulu. I'd like you to be home by the Fourth of July. When do you think you can get to Honolulu?

I don't know. Ask Noonan.

Amelia, please. Just give me a straight answer.

It's getting dark and his face is lit from below with the cool glow of the headlights. Up ahead there's a gate and a man at the gate and behind him a house in the distance. They're right next to the ocean now, it's gray and soft, and louder, always louder than she expects. She looks at the moon, which has just come up.

It looks like rain, she says.

He takes off his glasses and looks at

45

her. His dark irises flecked with yellow and green appear to be bleeding into the whites of his eyes. His face folds slightly with age and sadness.

We're here, she says.

They get out.

A man in uniform takes the keys from her and nods his head and drives the car away. She and G.P. walk up the gravel drive. It is lit with colored paper-covered lanterns. The ground is soft and it crunches with their steps, which are syncopated at first and then in unison.

We'll have to leave early so I can get some sleep.

I know. I've already . . .

Hello! Miss Earhart, George, so glad to see you. The guest of honor, please, right this way.

After dinner they walk down to the beach with their drinks and the women take their shoes off. The air is heavy with flowers and salt, and she walks next to Owen, who was at dinner. G.P. is in the house making a telephone call. The businessman and his wife and the rest of the guests are smoking and talking about a picture.

That one where Kate Hepburn plays a boy.

You didn't see it?

It was just awful.

Do you like her?

When she's all done up, I suppose.

Was Cary Grant in that?

Oh, yes, I saw it.

Their voices mix in and then out of the waves and eventually disappear. She and Owen walk along the flat plateau of sand. The water comes up to their ankles from time to time.

I heard you dropped the trailing wire, he says. His jacket is dangling from one finger. He's carrying his shoes in his hand.

It's too long. It's a nuisance.

Why didn't you tell me?

I didn't think it was important.

You know it's important. Your radio's no good without it. You won't get enough frequencies. You won't have the power.

I'm not worried about it. Your trousers are getting wet.

He bends down to cuff them and she looks at the water.

If you're not going to take the key transmitter, you'll need the trailing wire, he says.

It's not worth it to take the transmitter. You know I can't operate Morse code well enough. And I just told you, the trailing wire's too long. But don't worry about me. I'll be fine.

They walk in silence for a while.

They stop for a moment while she picks up a shell. She holds it to her ear.

It seems to me that you're being reckless. First Noonan. And now this, with the radio.

Maybe I am. Maybe it doesn't matter. She holds the cool shell up to his ear.

Don't say that, he says.

I have a feeling this time.

Don't say that.

All right. I won't.

They keep walking along, away from the house. They hear low swinging music playing. Across the road, behind a fringe of palms, people dancing on a veranda.

They stand for a moment in the calling night. The sky is aswarm with stars.

They stand for a while longer.

A man and a woman come walking down from the party. The woman laughs and the man is smoking. She kicks off her shoes, but he keeps his on. She grabs his hand and then lets it go. He holds his cigarette in his fingers, puts it back in his mouth, and looks out for a moment at the water. He is wearing a white dinner jacket and black pants. The woman runs ahead of him down to the water.

He waits because he sees two figures on the sand, and he watches them while he smokes. He drops his cigarette into the sand and he laughs and then he starts unlacing his shoes.

When Amelia catches sight of Noonan, he is following the woman to the water. He doesn't look down to where she and Owen are standing. He doesn't seem to have seen them. He takes off his jacket and then his shirt and then his pants and he walks into the water.

Some party, Owen says.

We should be getting back.

She leaves the shell on the sand and they head back.

Two days later, at dawn, she slips into the cockpit of her Electra. Noonan is in the rear cabin. G.P. climbs up onto the wing and kisses her before she closes the hatch. She pulls on her gloves. She waves one last wave. She starts the motor. It is already warm.

As the sun brushes up against the sky and lightness spreads out all around, she starts the motor. She signals to have the wheel chocks removed. She pulls down her goggles and adjusts them. She sees the puddles on the ground and the streaks of grease that float like rainbows on the surface of the puddles. She sees the shadows of the propellers begin to blur — and the light, she sees it changing on the surface of the puddles. She sees the mechanics and the others back away from the plane. She sees their feet step gingerly backward.

When she pulls out, the crowd that has assembled at the field surges violently forward, knocking over three policemen. Women fan themselves to keep from fainting. A photographer scrambles up a fence. In the center of it all, her plane gleams dully, like a barge of beaten silver. It glides down the runway and it stops and it turns and the crowd tenses and even she has to catch her breath. She is alone in the cockpit, alone with the sky ahead of her. She catches sight of Owen, in the distance, riffling through the pages of his notebook. He takes a pen from his pocket. He scribbles in his notebook: 5:56, *the dawn, breaking.* Then the engine revs up and kicks in and it builds and she is alive inside the color of the sky.

It's not long after we take off that I realize what a mistake I've made. It's not long, but it's too late. What I understand right away is that I'll never go to New York again. Why I think of New York, I don't know. It occurs to me that I have walked through Central Park for the last time.

Never again will I see the tops of those trees, burnished, on fire, lost to me.

Three

It was a demented trip. The entire journey, flying as fast as possible like fugitive angels, took more than a month, during which time we spent our days feverish from the flaming sun or lost in the artillery of monsoon rains and almost always astonished by the unearthly architecture of the sky. In spite of the hazardous conditions, or perhaps because of them, Noonan drank and I flew with reckless, melodramatic abandon, and as the voyage progressed we carelessly flung overboard any pretense of civility. Much later, when I looked back on the flight, it seemed to me that we had been two lost souls in an immense netherworld, traveling toward an arbitrary goal, wondering which of us was more forsaken: the navigator who didn't care where we were going, or the pilot who didn't care if we ever got there.

* * *

We must have both known that we shared something, a secret craving for oblivion. But there is no such thing as oblivion. Oblivion is a lie.

They climb slowly. For thirteen minutes, they climb slowly, and then they swing in the direction of Puerto Rico. Underneath them the water is a pale, pure green, and underneath that the sand is white. The gauzy shapes of giant fish swim over the sand like clouds above the desert.

At six o'clock she tunes in to WQAM. They will be broadcasting the weather conditions every half hour. When she tunes in they are sending out a description of her takeoff. She listens in suspense and smiles. It is hot in the cockpit and so she takes off her jacket. She hears that she has gotten off safely.

Dawn turns to day and the light grows hazy. A few clouds glide under the Electra's wings, like swans under a bridge. The shadows of the clouds draw giant petals and paw prints on the surface of the pale-green sea.

In San Juan, a Miss Montgomery, the

only private flyer on the island and a wild beauty who smokes thin cigars, puts them up for the night. At dusk she drives them to her sugarcane plantation. Along the way they pass banana trees and breadfruit trees and pineapple growing along the ground. They drive along a road that smells like coffee and she explains that they are driving through a coffee plantation. Miss Montgomery is smoking one of her thin cigars, and she talks with it in her mouth.

I have sixteen hundred acres, she says.

They are suitably impressed.

The car bumps along a dirt road up to her house, past field after field of sugarcane. Along the side of the road there are wildflowers, and parrots up in the trees. Up ahead they see her house, which is painted white, with a balcony of bougainvillea. Behind it the sea appears to rise straight up, like a backdrop of bright blue sky.

With the help of a bottle of rum made from her own cane, Miss Montgomery persuades Noonan to play dominoes on the veranda.

Ice, Mr. Noonan?

No, thank you.
Your move.
Yes, my move.

Later, in a room with a view of the sea, she is awakened by the sound of laughter coming from another room, Miss Montgomery's room. She recognizes Noonan's low, dark laugh. It is a laugh that has liquor in it.

The next day when they take off he's hungover and half asleep. She's furious when they land nineteen minutes behind schedule. She threatens to have someone else sent for the job, immediately, before she leaves the continent. But he persuades her to keep him. He says it won't happen again. He smiles his smile. He is very persuasive.

On good days we groped through clouds that hung down like dirty laundry, and slept on flattened mattresses in one of our many exotic ports of call. But more often we suffered through schizophrenic weather and spent the night in hangars, on rancid cots with sinister stains, in the shadow of our battered ship.

One night we were staying in a hotel,

the Palace Hotel. We ran into an old friend of his, a radio operator. The two of them spent the whole night drinking. I came downstairs at three in the morning and found him drinking at the hotel bar. I was wearing my nightgown and my flight jacket.

What do you think you're doing? I said.

I'm dictating my will, he said.

We have to be on the airfield in two hours, I said.

You are a magnificent creature, he said.

It doesn't take long for him to realize that flying with her isn't like flying with other pilots. Sometimes when she is angry she plays hide-and-seek with the clouds, looking for weather to cheer her up. She likes to drop a thousand feet in a matter of seconds. She seems to have no fear. It terrifies him and makes him sick. When they land he pukes on the runway, right next to the plane, and curses her under his acrid breath.

She returns his lack of faith in her with her own judgment: she decides that he is a coward. At night, victim to the fires in his brain, he tosses and turns and flinches in his sleep like an animal roasting on a spit. His feet stick out one end of the short blanket. She notices that he's afraid to clip his long, lethal toenails because he doesn't want to cut himself, and this makes her worry about his ability to perform his demanding job.

But he always recovers from his late nights and alcohol just in time to accompany her to their social obligations, guiding her with arch looks and bemused glances through the maze of unfamiliar people and places. At every stop they are received by local dignitaries, acting governors general and local welcoming committees. Lunch is usually prepared by a team of expatriate wives, and it usually consists of something like beefsteak and grape juice and apple pie, for these women are eager to cook a patriotic meal. There is usually someone official who sits next to Amelia. The wives sit on either side of Noonan and cut his steak.

On one of our stops Noonan visited a fortune-teller, whose psychic powers amazed him. Alarmed by nightmares I had been having in which the Electra fell violently out of the sky, I also went to consult with her. The runes said that there was nothing in my future to prevent a long and happy life, and that prediction gave me hope. Exhilarated by the possibility that we would complete our journey, I decided to assume full command of my ship. That was how the battle of wills between me and Noonan stopped being an amateur match of pussyfooting and became obsessive and more intense than ever. We argued openly, we threw off the mantle of decorum, and we engaged in long-winded tirades strung with pornographic curses that offended even the airfield mechanics who didn't speak any English.

He was afraid of her lack of fear, and she was frightened by his cowardice. The more he drank, the more reckless she became; the more reckless she became, the more he drank. Crazy, they both were. No one had ever had access to their madness, ever really noticed it, but for them it was ordinary, a necessity.

* * *

Later, as we settled into some semblance of a routine, Noonan drank and I flew with less and less inhibition. Soaring blindly over the blank page of the barren desert, we puzzled over the elusive landmarks described on our indecipherable land maps: *In the bed of the Wadi Howar two heglig trees about four hundred meters apart were ring-barked. They mark the intersection of the twenty-fourth meridian.* In a stupor of intoxication and heedless freedom, we lost ourselves in the arid romance of the places over which we flew — Qala-en Hahl, Umm Shiayshin, Abu Seid, Idd el Bashir. And we let ourselves be mesmerized like religious fanatics by the waves of heat dancing off the rippling sand and by the silence that blanketed the bleakest stretches, where every now and then a caravan trail led off to nowhere, or a camp with a tent or two stood out from its surroundings like a mockery of survival.

We became voyeurs of the intimate relationship between wind and sand. We watched the air draw fine lines on the surface of the desert and make wrinkles in the face of the wasteland.

We saw a dust storm whip the ground into the air until the world disappeared from sight. Later, in the aftermath of the apocalypse, ominous black eagles appeared out of nowhere, winging around us, like carpetbaggers hoping to benefit from the devastation of a war. During this time we spent many hours without exchanging a word, and this, probably more than anything else, is what brought us closest together. We saw the same sights and felt the same breezes. We watched the same sun and the same moon dip in and out of the same clouds. We felt the same rain and heard the same silences. It was like sharing a dream with someone else. For a little while, we were as peaceful as two angels riding a tandem bicycle, cruising through the heavens, and for days I did not think about the pestilential odor of Noonan's breath or the suicidal candor with which I had ignored my own safety. Instead I dreamed of nothing but porcelain clouds cascading in slow-motion waterfalls against a backdrop of robin's-egg blue.

None of our dreaming was in vain. The reverie we fell into from Khartoum to

Karachi helped alleviate our fear of crashing in the desert, and then, when we least expected it, we arrived safely in Calcutta. Approaching the metropolis, we saw factories and little villages, and we had the feeling of returning to civilization. It was not the most benign sensation, however, and it brought with it a suspicion that amidst the trappings of society, however foreign, we would be unable to continue our truce. And that is exactly what happened.

The pilot touched down at Dum-Dum airport, and on the way into the city, passing through wide streets, as they caught sight of a marquee showing Shirley Temple in *Captain January*, she and her navigator began to bicker.

They picked up their arguing just where they had left it, with a discussion of Noonan's hypocritical fastidiousness, a lecture on the way he brushed his hair ten times as often as his teeth, and an appendix on the way he insisted on carefully folding his dirty clothes. In the days that followed, he was told that his vaguely southern accent sounded phony, and that she didn't believe he didn't realize that he had one. He was made aware that as a partner in her flirtation with death, it was incumbent upon him never to remark on the risks they were taking or on the unlikelihood of their success, even in good fun. Good fun, in fact, was a tender subject; she hated his sense of humor. If he tried to tease her, she acted wounded and offended. If he tried to cheer her up, she said his jokes were bad. He found this last stab of hostility cruel. He could be very funny; other people had told him so. He assumed it was just another twist in the barbed wire of their connection and made a halfhearted effort to forgive her for it.

On one occasion, however, her game-playing had infuriated him, nearly ending their journey in the middle.

It had started off innocently enough: they were on the road to Mandalay. A monsoon had brought them down early from Akyab on their way to Bangkok, and after two hours of sightless flying through soupy weather they had landed in Rangoon. A Mr. Austin C. Brady, the American consul, met them at the airfield and offered to take them sightseeing. The rain was pouring down heavily and the prognosis was for more of the same, so they decided it would be hazardous to continue on and accepted his generosity. In the car he pointed out places of interest along the way and maneuvered past various animals. The road on which they were driving was called Mandalay, and he told them that it was, as a matter of fact, the very road made famous by Kipling's poem. In the heart of the city the streets were thronged, and Mr. Brady proudly identified the Burmese, Hindus, Muslims, Christians, and Chinese by their varying dress, habits, and language. Gharries clopped by, pulled by single horses and shuttered against the rain. Rickshaw runners sped past on foot, kicking up sprays of mud. The runners wore conical coolie hats made of old kerosene tins. Mr. Brady commented that he thought these must be noisy in the rain, but that they were the custom, and then he shrugged.

From the air their first sight of Rangoon had been the gold spire of the Shwe Dagon Pagoda. Now, as they approached the shrine by car, the rain let up and the sun broke through the clouds. It dried off the glistening roof, which pointed like an elongated nipple up to the heavens. Worshipers moved purposefully in and out of the temple, an elaborate structure apparently made up of many different buildings. There was an air of spiritual business about the place, not too ethereal, but not too worldly. A long arcade covered with graded roofs, each poking up behind the one before it like houses on a steep hillside, led up to the interior of the shrine. Raindrops dripped off the high palm leaves. A spicy thread of incense wafted through the air. Mr. Brady stepped out of the car and lit a cigar. They followed him and stood for a moment, just staring at the majesty of the pagoda.

Then she said, Well, we have to go up.

Of course, Noonan answered, sure.

They headed to the entrance of the covered staircase at a time during which Mr. Brady was too engrossed in his smoke to explain to them the etiquette of the temple. As soon as they reached the foot of the stairs, however, an old man in a silk dress who appeared to be dead in his chair jumped up and started explaining to them in international gibberish that they would have to remove their shoes. That the shrine could only be entered barefoot. She leaned over and unlaced her sensible brown oxfords, and then she took off her socks. She began making her way up the steps, but when she reached the sixth one she turned around and saw Noonan, still at the bottom, staring up at her with an expression of forced cheeriness.

Go ahead without me, he called up. I've changed my mind. I'll stay here.

Never in his life had he received such a stupefied look. And miss the pagoda? she said.

It took several minutes, during which she refused to descend from her position of self-righteous elevation, for him to get around to confessing that he didn't want to take off his shoes. It was probably the most difficult moment of their journey together. She could not abide his refusal to take off his shoes, and her intolerance enraged him. As she stood there on the steps, worshipers on their way up and down passing her on either side, some pausing to take in the spectacle of two undignified Americans, she argued with him about the merits of seeing the shrine, the wastefulness of missing it, the prudish-ness of modesty, and the beauty of the human foot. The more she said, the angrier he became, and the more deter-mined not to take off his shoes. She seemed to him to be intentionally and maliciously dragging him as far away from Nirvana as possible, and he told her so. This was his great mistake. She turned around. She walked slowly up the steps. She spent an hour and a half in the shrine.

For three days we didn't speak. It was the last three days before Lae. Then in Lae, New Guinea, our last stop before Howland Island, the wind was blowing the wrong way.

Four

Lae. It seems the farthest precinct of human habitation. Tall, rocky islands reach up from the ocean like the mortified fingers of the dead. The sky is filled with billowing cloud beasts. In the shallow waters, thatch-roofed huts wobble on stilts like long-legged insects. The runway is a thin strip cleared through the jungle. It ends on a cliff hanging over the sea. In the local pidgin English, all the women are called Mary. The wind is blowing the wrong way.

She is surprised that Noonan doesn't seem outwardly troubled by the weather, and she has no sense from him that he is even thinking about the dangers that lie ahead. She is struck with the sudden fear that he has given up all hope, but she puts aside her anxieties because in spite of his drinking, she secretly harbors the suspicion that he is brave.

The truth is that Noonan is sure that they are going to die. It is this certainty that accounts for his outward calm, as he watches in silence for any sign that his intuition is faulty. But the ominous winds rage on. She has radioed the *Itasca*, a Coast Guard cutter posted to listen for her signals and watch for weather. The meteorological forecast cites squalls and headwinds. They need good weather because Noonan needs good star sights. Their only hope of finding Howland Island is by celestial navigation. But the odds are worse than terrible. Because of radio difficulties, Noonan hasn't been able to set the chronometers, and any miscalculation of their speed would defeat the accuracy of navigating by the stars. His gyroscope has been unreliable over the past week. And she has to gauge her fuel consumption, but the fuel analyzer has been off, first in India and then in Indonesia.

The *Itasca* is supposed to help guide them to Howland, but the captain doesn't know that she has left her telegraph code key transmitter in Miami. Incredible as it seems, neither she nor Noonan knows how to communicate in Morse code. The captain is also unaware that she has dropped her trailing wire, the antenna that would allow her to broadcast and receive signals on more frequencies.

Later, when they discover how mismanaged the flight has been, people will think that she was out of her mind.

He couldn't sleep. He went to wander along the water, reciting prayers into the howling wind. That night he drank himself into a stupor, and when he staggered into his room he fell onto the bed, not noticing that it was covered in mosquito netting. The structure collapsed. The clamor woke her up. When she helped him back into bed, she told him that they would be leaving the next morning.

He said that it wasn't up to her. It was up to the fucking wind.

They left the next day. The Electra waddled off the end of the cliff and disappeared for several seconds. Then she rose up from the water like a Phoenix, only to disappear again, into the ashen mist.

Behind the mist, there's nothing but sky. The sky is flesh. It's the last sky.

I'm flying around the world. I'm flying over the Pacific somewhere off the coast of New Guinea in my twin-engine Lockheed Electra, and I'm lost. I watch the sky as it curves and swells, and every now and then I think I can see it shudder. My eyes and my eyes reflected in the windshield hold the sun in them, and it burns. I blink and reach one arm directly overhead. My fingers grasp a dial. Out of the far corner of my field of vision, I catch a glimpse of the underlying sea. Thinking to myself that this might be the last day of my life, that I'm hot, and that I am hungry, I adjust the dial and lower my arm.

The sea is dark. It is darker than the sky.

Earhart. Overcast.

We must be on you but cannot see you.

Earhart calling *Itasca*. We are circling but cannot hear you.

72

* * *

The navigator has been roused from his stupor and is drinking from the bottle of rum. He stands up slowly and immediately sits down. He moans and then closes his eyes.

While he awakes, night falls. One by one the stars arrive in the sky like a thousand distant windows lighting up. Soon the emptiness is crowded with heavenly bodies, crowded with glitter and smothered in moonlight.

He picks up a bottle and sets it on the map, a beacon for lost mariners. He looks out the window and studies the stars. Then he scribbles some calculations on the map itself, filling up the ocean with ink. He rips off a corner of the map and writes a note, which he attaches to a string hanging from the bamboo pole. He pulls on the string and the note travels forward into the cockpit. Then he sits back and opens the bottle.

He waits a long time for a response, and while he waits, he makes the liquor last. It isn't his only bottle; he's hidden more somewhere, but for the moment he can't remember where. The drink takes hold. In the awareness of lost awareness, he feels that he is able to see his mind in motion, and this fascinates him. It's like being inside a watch.

It is this very passivity and self-absorption that she hates about his drinking. He has a hard time deciding if he agrees with her. He's suffered for his habit over the years, sometimes more painfully than he can admit, and he realizes that this has made his life difficult. But then again, if his life hadn't been difficult to begin with, he wouldn't have been drinking anyway. He never takes the argument very far. It's a subject he can only contemplate when drunk.

The handsome navigator is dreaming about a pair of stockinged legs, light glossing over silk over pearly skin, when he remembers that he has been waiting for a reply from the cockpit.

He stands up slowly and immediately sits down. He moans and closes his eyes. He stands up again, and balancing his weight on the table, he steadies himself and heads for the cockpit.

Much later, when Noonan remembers

what happened, he will flatter himself by recalling that as soon as he sat down in the copilot's seat, he had a premonition of death.

In reality, when he sees the thin margin of error left on the fuel gauge and hears the blind static sputter weakly from the radio, he has a vision of escape involving feathers and wings. Then he steadies his wits and takes off his glasses, one wire over one ear at a time, and he squeezes the bridge of his nose. He's obviously nervous. His hand trembles. His confusion — he has no idea where they are or how they have drifted so far off course — hardens into a carapace of false self-control. Gesturing out the window with one hand while he puts on his glasses with the other, he says, The United States is that way, remember?

When she doesn't answer or look over at him, he asks her what the hell is going on. He reaches down toward the dashboard to fiddle with the radio, and in her first statement to him in what is beginning to feel like days, she tells him that it doesn't work. He asks her again what the hell is going on.

What the hell do you think is going on.

The mindless roar of the engine is interrupted by a rattling, and then by a thumping sound.

Jesus, he says. What the hell is going on? What the goddamn hell is going on?

The thumping increases, and then suddenly it changes. It slows to a rumble. Then down to a purr.

Jesus, he says again. Jesus goddamn Christ. Why won't you tell me what the hell is going on?

As they descend she can feel the full weight of her ship barreling beneath her. It is a soaring, howling fall. She comes reeling out of the sky like some wanton satellite winging her way reckless and unhinged. Her metal skeleton scrapes the atmosphere which seems to rupture as she passes, healing behind her as she passes, sucking her through again and again. She feels the shaking of her brakes and the shivering of her wings in a sweeping passage down to where she lingers for a moment in the moonlit darkness, the sea below her as black as blood. For a moment, everything asway. The silent waves. The hot, salt air. The wind holding, holding her up before letting her go. Then a cracking and a breaking and a last long shudder as she speeds down into the final chaos.

He grabbed onto her, sobbing, when he felt the fall. He clutched her hair and he gasped for breath. She carried the weight of him in her arms, letting the tears roll down her neck, and she thought about the weakness of men. She felt weak herself, but not too frightened to face the night and everything it offered, even if what it offered was only death. They were both dying ridiculous deaths, she thought, brought about by hubris and liquor. They might as well have been lovers, she thought. They had made all the blunders of a typical couple: he had woken up from the dream too late, and she was too angry to forgive him for his absence. It was tragic, but life was tragic, especially the mysterious entanglements of men and women. She had never given much thought to relations between the sexes, she had always tried to live her own life. But now here she was, on the brink of the abyss, with a grown man collapsed in her arms. It was fate and it was funny and it was making her angry. She was filled with regret for not having been kinder to him, and she burned with a desire to start their journey over from the beginning, but she couldn't forgive him for everything he'd done, and she blamed him more than herself for her circumstances. She wished she could say something comforting to him, but she couldn't, and then she wished that he would pull himself together.

She looked over his shoulder out the window at the night, and she saw the strange constellations, empty and meaningful, strung like jewels. She wanted to live, but it occurred to her that death might be just as beautiful as flying.

I'm sorry, he said finally. This was all my fault.

Don't be an idiot, she said.

Part Two

To day we love what to morrow
    we hate;
To day we seek what to morrow
    we shun;
To day we desire what to morrow
    we fear,
nay, even tremble at the
    apprehensions of . . .
        — DANIEL DEFOE, *Robinson Crusoe*

Five

When she wakes from the lucid dream that carries her three thousand feet down, in a tumbling parade of images from the farthest reaches of her memory, her first impression will be that she has died a violent death and gone directly to hell.

A barely perceptible change comes over her, a heightened sense of awareness enters her, the moonlight on the ocean turns from blue to silver, an infinitesimal change. Everything inside her shifts slightly too, shifts from one shade to another.

Never again will I see New York. Never again will I drive my silver Cord Phaeton. From now on I'll only have Noonan and my Electra, and I'll live on a desert island. And I'll be lost in the between, in the emptiness of the between, with the threats and the moments of radiant danger, the perfect days, the oases, the furious whisper of the night wind in the trees, the happiness, my fears, the imminent dawn.

She moved. Her neck was stiff but it felt good to move it. She turned to her right, and without saying anything she looked at Noonan. He started talking. He said it was a miracle. He said she'd saved his life. She listened without saying anything. He went on. He said this couldn't be Howland Island but that maybe they were not far off. He said maybe they'd died and gone to heaven. She didn't say anything for a long time because she was convinced that she had lost her ability to speak. But she did stare out the windshield at the astonishing view, a heartbreaking dawn over glittering waters, and it looked real enough to persuade her she was alive.

It went very quickly, those first few days. They got out of the plane, and together they looked around and tried to make sense of their surroundings. Then all of a sudden, as if part of the choreography of a dream, they set about performing the necessary rituals of survival.

They check the radio, which picks up nothing, and the fuel tank, which is low but not empty, and they confirm their worst suspicions — that they have no idea where they are. They do have some gas left; it seems impossible, but it is true. The fuel analyzer malfunctioned, and she managed to land before the Electra lost everything. They build a fire on the beach to attract attention. They know that a search will have already begun. They construct two water-collection tanks out of cloth fuel covers, and Noonan begins experimenting with ways of turning salt water into fresh. He builds a small device which collects the water as it evaporates and funnels it back into a deep shell. But the process is painstakingly slow. They use the bamboo fishing pole to catch their dinner, and after dinner they let the fire burn all night.

It's a small island. Not even an island really, more of an atoll, four miles long and half a mile wide. It isn't much more than a sandbar. There's an outer ring of coral reef that extends from the beach about five hundred feet at low tide, and an inner ring of jungle encircling a peaceful lagoon. The fringes of the reef are infested by sharks that appear every evening promptly at five. The beach is lined with coconut palms which sway lazily in the wind and spill their bounty on the sand. The jungle is a labyrinth of immense, muscular, twisted stalks in the midst of which rats make their hairy nests, spiders spin enormous webbed cathedrals, and gargantuan coconut crabs remain motionless for days. Unlike the islands she had read about in her youth, this one did not have tattooed natives drumming around bonfires, but the lagoon was enchanting, complete with exotic flowers and technicolor fishes, and a perfumed, paradisal air. She had not bothered to explore the place the very instant they arrived, as someone else stranded on a desert island might have done immediately. Instead she became aware of her environment gradually in the days to come, first discovering the lagoon at sunset when she had lost herself in the maze of the jungle while looking for a good place to urinate and saw, through the silken death net of a spider's web, the light making pink and yellow lily pads on the undulating surface of the water.

She knows that she wanted this to happen. She made it happen. But she never expected it to happen. She has nothing with her but a change of clothes, the dictionary of pidgin English she bought in Lae, and her silver powder compact. She left behind a parachute, a life raft, her good-luck elephant's foot bracelet, and in order to make the plane as light as possible, they had unloaded anything else deemed unessential on the runway in New Guinea. She hadn't even wanted Noonan to take the pearl-handled knife he had bought in a street market in Dakar, but now she is grateful for it because it enables her to hack through the otherwise impenetrable jungle.

The first night, she and Noonan sleep next to each other on the beach. The sky is clear, the sea is calm, the wide night stretches out like an enormous tent, but still she is troubled by the sound of his breathing, by his nocturnal mutterings, and by the feeling that on this loneliest of islands she is unfortunately not alone.

She reveals herself to him in her despair. In the middle of the night she gets up from their makeshift camp and in her ravaged sleep she climbs into the Electra. She climbs into the plane, which sits on the reef flat like an embodiment of their grounded longings. She sits, her hands lightly skimming the controls, her eyes focused past the darkness over the sea. She sits in a meditation so intense that for a moment even he believes that she is flying through a supernatural element.

The plane doesn't move. A seagull perches on top of it, mocking its directionless, stationary flight.

Already, in the sky, she was preparing for these mysterious, internal flights.

The sky, now I know, is endless.

Very soon, fortunately, it rains. After the rain she sits by the lagoon and watches the giant frogs relaxing on sunbaked stones, their mouths popping open to catch bugs. She watches flocks of migrating birds rise like plumes of lavender smoke across the ocean at twilight. She admires the sharks, their punctual appointments with death, the leisurely circles they make in the sea. In one day she sees them devour three exotic birds which dip down to the water for dinner. First the purple one was pulled under by a sudden force, and then the other two disappeared in a clean swipe, and then all that was left were a few iridescent feathers swirling gently in a bloody whirlpool.

The streamlined precision of the sharks makes her long for the fluid engineering of her plane.

These are very good, he says.

We don't talk much, but then one day he asks me if I like coconut. I tell him, somewhat formally, because I haven't been speaking much, that I have never been introduced to coconut.

I never met one I didn't like, he says.

He hands me a coconut, teases me. I look at it. I turn it around and around, the liquid splashing inside. I wonder how to get at it. It's like a human head, maddening, inaccessible.

You have to shell a coconut to get at its fruit, and for that you need a machete. I don't know that, so I try to break it on a tree. I hit the tree with it, but nothing happens. When I throw the coconut at the tree again, we both start to laugh. Then I throw the coconut at him, and he catches it, and he falls backward, still laughing. He takes his knife out from his pocket and starts to shell the fruit. When he splits open the white skull, the milk drips over, and I realize how hungry I am. We've been eating fish and drinking the water we collected, but I realize that I'm hungry for something sweet.

I notice that for the first time I'm noticing him.

He says he feels sorry for me because I've never eaten a coconut before. Never had the experience, he says. I say I don't need his pity and anyway here I am, about to taste a coconut. He hands me half the coconut to drink from, and I take it, the liquid almost painful it's so sugary. I feel it travel from my mouth all over my body. He asks me if I like it. But I don't hear him at first; I'm just looking at him and listening to the sea. He asks me again and before I can answer he hands me another piece. I feel something deepen inside me, very gently, like the sand soaking up the water after a wave. I feel that I've absorbed something.

Sometimes the sound of the ocean is almost deafening. It's like the roar of the Electra's engine. I remember some things so vividly: the light was bright, but now it's falling, the beach is empty, we don't speak, we're surrounded by the continuous roar of the ocean, we're swept up in it, borne along. There are no obstacles between us and the water, just the sand, and then the reef, and then the sea. Out on the water you can see the shadows of the clouds going by under the slanting sunlight. Great masses of clouds sometimes. They look like the undersides of vast ships. Their shadows look like ships on the water. The wind can be as deafening as the water, and the sound of trees in the wind is frightening. Palm leaves can make a noise more portentous than anything I've ever heard. It's a sound of rage, full of heat.

Now the day is ending. You can tell by the water, the tide's coming back in again. It's coming home at the end of the day, reaching closer and closer.

The beach is separated from the sea

by the coral reef flat, which the water is beginning to cover. There's nothing separating us from the ocean. It doesn't know that we exist, although we watch it all day. It surrounds us, rules our lives, cuts us off, brings us together, holds us.

The smell of the lagoon drifts by in the late air, and the smells of salty water, coconut flesh, birds, sweat, flowers, strange spices, fire, the fire always burning on the lonely stretch of beach. The smell of the island is the smell of the sea and the desert and the jungle mixed into one.

I find him sitting in the back of the plane. He's drinking rum, smoking one of his last cigarettes.

He says what took me so long, he's been waiting for me. I've been listening to the sea. He is lit on one side by moonlight streaming in through the window.

He's a very predictable man, for a drunk. I bet he comes here often. This must already be part of his routine, I think. He's an addict. He's addicted to his habits, to his drink, to his cigarettes. He was addicted to women. He must still be addicted to women.

We look at each other in the blue light. The air is an eerie, nightclub blue. It lends everything a sordid drama. He smells strongly of good rum, cheap tobacco, burning wood, salt — he smells wonderful. He's drunk and he asks me to stay awhile. Pull up a chair, he says.

He tells me that he thinks we're going to be saved, and then he tells me we are going to die here. He talks to me, tells me he knew from the beginning this would happen, that he knew when we were crossing the ocean, crossing the desert, he knew that I would take him to this place. Now, he says, I'll probably leave him to die here alone, I'll betray him somehow. He says the fortune-teller told him he would live a long, happy life. I told him she said that to me too. We laugh and then he becomes quiet, brooding. I close my eyes and smell his smell. He's used to it, I know, the effect he has on women. But I don't believe this is the usual effect.

Later, we make love very easily, half asleep. It's understood that it doesn't mean anything.

The sound of the water is so intimate,

so close, you can hear it lapping underneath the Electra. It feels as if we're on a ship anchored at sea. I touch his hair in the darkness. The moon is obscured. The clouds pass over it in black, lacy veils.

I wake him up and tell him I need to talk to him. I need to talk so that I don't lose my mind. Tell me a story, I say. Tell me what we'll say to the reporters when they bring us back to New York.

He felt for the bottle of rum and gave it to me. Very softly, right in my hair, he spoke to me.

He told me what we would say when we got back to New York.

Because I want to be close to him but don't know how, I say something I don't entirely mean. I want to tell him something nice so I say to him, Thank you, that was a good story.

It's the middle of the night. He says they'll never believe us if we tell them the truth. He says maybe we should keep it a secret. We'll tell them that we were taken by pirates, or by the Japanese, and captured as spies. He tells me that he's never been anywhere like this, and I say, I know, neither have I.

I still remember his story. I remember the way he told it, just what words he used. It was a story about spying on the Japanese and being captured and tortured and executed. But he told it in a very funny way, using fake voices and giving characters silly names. At one point he used an expression I'd never heard: "rearranging deck chairs on the *Titanic*." It seemed at once too silly and too sophisticated for him, but I realize he is actually a very sophisticated, very rough, contradictory man.

It was a sad story, but it ended with a happy twist. I thanked him for it, told him it was a good story, and then he asked me what I was really thinking.

At night I dream about my plane. I see myself sinking to the bottom of the ocean in my once magnificent Electra, my eyes focused blankly on the perpetual blue, my silk scarf floating in an eternal wave. Later, a man with a hat appears to me. He's standing on the coral reef flat in the dawn, his tie lifting in the wind, a silver Cord Phaeton parked behind him, waiting to take me away. The first dream calms me. It seems perfectly natural. The second one wakes me up. It's a nightmare.

Morning streams in through the windows. The specially installed windows of the navigator's cabin. They've spent the night in the Electra, almost by accident, and now it's hot inside, a furnace.

They leave the plane. She's put on her silk scarf, knotted it loosely around her neck, and powdered her sunburnt nose. She knows she's behaving with a comic degree of civility, but it's the way she's always responded to disaster. There's a new lightness to her actions now, a desperate comedy.

He sees it and he says, Your nose looks fine.

The first couple of days have gone by and I've forgotten how angry I was at him. I'm still in shock. He's very kind to me. He seems to feel he owes me his life because somehow I was able to land the Electra on a reef flat. I, on the other hand, I blame him for our situation. If not for him, I think, we would be home. But then when I think that, I'm not sure whether to blame him or to say, No, it's you who saved my life. But I don't feel that yet. I don't thank him. I won't feel that for quite a while.

I ask him to tell me about his life. I don't really know anything about him. He says he's spent so many years trying to forget it, he's not sure he can tell his story. It started when he went to sea, at fifteen; he was a kitchen boy. He went around the world in ships, many times. Once he was held in Madagascar for forty-five days. He grew up in those forty-five days, fell in love, had love, fell out of love. He learned about the stars in his years at sea, he knows how to read the stars.

That's all you really need to know about me, he says, I know how to read the stars.

I ask about the stars, if he can tell us where we are. He has some idea, but his calculations don't make sense. He was passed out for so much of our last leg that he lost track of where we were. He was drunk when we took off. He was certain we were going to die. When we left, the wind was blowing the wrong way. He says that on the airfield, when we unloaded the plane, my scarf dancing hysterically in the air, he says then he knew we were going to die. He says it as if he had been right, as if his fear were a legitimate excuse.

You were afraid, I say, but you were wrong.

I wasn't wrong to be afraid, he says. It was the wind that did us in.

Suddenly I feel sick. It's a slight dizziness, a subtle unbalancing. It's my heart, sinking, when I realize that I am alone. He's so afraid, I remember, and all the anger returns. I don't have time to feel compassionate. Here I am, alone again, alone but not completely by myself, alone without the freedom of not having to think about someone else. Suddenly all the anger that washed away in the trance of our landing reappears, and I wish that Noonan had died. I don't hear what he's saying, I just watch him talking, and instead of his dark beauty, I see his eyes: they're filled with fear. He sees that I'm seeing him and he stops talking, but I recover, pretend I'm listening. He says he thinks maybe he can use the engine to charge up the radio and try to make contact with passing ships, or something like that. I say it wasn't the wind that did us in. He doesn't seem to have heard me.

This is how we talk to each other now, in overlapping monologues. We've been separated by fear. Fear has set in, and memory, and blame. I'm awake most of the night, waiting for a ship to see our fire, hearing in the wind the voice of the radio operator, hearing the scratch of his breath in the shifting leaves, comforting myself in my anguish with memory traces, the agonizing moments before I lost contact with the world.

Then I dream of my Electra and wake up shaking.

It's always this way: the worst times are when I'm reminded that I can no longer fly. When I wake up, when the tide is out, when Noonan is asleep, I go and sit in the cockpit whose every inch I know by heart. I sit under the light of a starry sky, illegible to me but sparkling so clearly it seems a different sky than the ones I've known before, written in an intricately beautiful foreign language, and the flights that I have made in the past retain their original magic when I reenact them in my mind.

She sits, her fingers touching the familiar dials, her body shaking slightly in response to an imaginary motion, her mind projecting scenes of deserts and cities on the screen of her closed eyes.

After these flights she's overcome by an unbearable sadness. And then in the morning, her anger at Noonan returns.

Six

Our daily life revolved around the dinners on the beach. When he tells me that he started off as a kitchen boy on a ship, I tell him that he has to cook me dinner, and he does, every night, on the beach.

The evenings are long and empty. He prepares fish when he can catch them, but he hasn't found the best spots yet, the fertile inlets, and so some nights he comes up with nothing, not even a crab, and we're so hungry in our desperation that he cooks what he can find. One night it's a rat. The meat is thin and stringy, tasteless, and he waits awhile to tell me that it's a rat, as if I haven't noticed it isn't a fish. He tries to make conversation with me, but I'm furious. Not about the rat, but about the flight, about his fear. I think that I'm angry at him because he's afraid, as if that's something to be angry about. I blame everything on him and it makes it worse for me. He can't hold all my anger. After dinner, I clear away the bones, the ashes, in a silent and inexplicable rage. He seems wounded, not surprisingly, and he tries to tell the story of his adventures at sea, or on the Mississippi as a riverboat captain. I'm inconsolable. I treat him more brutally than I've ever treated anyone.

Later, he keeps talking to me, trying to make conversation.

You know your husband, he says.

G.P.? I say.

Yes, well, him. You know I never liked him, he says.

Oh really, why not?

I thought he was silly, he says. I thought that he didn't understand you.

Well he didn't, I say to the ocean. But you don't either.

He drinks. He rations his liquor. He pours it out into a coconut shell. I watch him. The first time, I remember, he measured and measured, and then he filled the shell up to the top. I almost started laughing, after his careful measurements.

How did you get to be such a stinking drunk? I ask.

Two ways, he says. Gradually and then suddenly.

He drinks it all. He doesn't offer me any. I don't thank him for dinner, he doesn't thank me for cleaning up. We are like prisoners, convicts.

Eventually, I stop saying anything about his drinking. I don't feel that I can; I've maintained some obscure sense of etiquette, because my life no longer depends on his ability to keep sober and do his job. Although now, in a sense, it matters more. We have to keep the fires burning and stay on the lookout for passing ships, always the dream of passing ships. We are still expecting to be rescued. We don't say anything about it to each other, but it is the religion that gives our days direction. It's taken for granted that we will survive this, that we'll be home one day, away from each other, released, that we have separate futures, that we can treat each other however we please, it doesn't matter, we don't matter to each other. This is because we are still dreaming, still falling. We haven't yet landed. We barely speak to each other anymore, except to exchange factual information. One night after dinner, when he's drinking, by now he's already drunk, he tells me that he's seen a plane. At first I pretend I haven't heard. He doesn't repeat what he's said, and I don't ask. These are the rules of our bloodless warfare. We're silent for a while, long enough for me to forget what he's said, and then, once I've written it off as a drunken slur and forgotten it completely, only then, only then do I hear something terrifying. It's a faint, unnatural, mechanical hum. It's a painfully familiar yet utterly foreign sound. After I hear it, there's a second of silence. Everything seems to stop. I remember what Noonan said. I hate him more than ever. We put more wood on the fire. We wait on the beach. It's dark, and we don't see anything.

In the middle of the night I go to the Electra for one of my midnight voyages. But by the time I get there, I've woken up completely, I'm no longer in a trance. I'm awake and I walk into the navigator's cabin. In my bare feet I walk on our charts, our maps, scraps of paper covered with calculations. Noonan's shoes are lying in a corner. I open up one of the drawers in his table and I find that it is filled with bottles of rum. I don't even try to stop myself. I take out the bottles, I leave the Electra. I walk down to the beach. It's very dark, the moon is dim, and I walk to the edge of the water. I look out into the darkness. I'm looking for a plane, a sign, a glimmer, anything. It's completely dark. The air is heavy, and hot, it won't rain yet. I open the bottles. I take a sip from one of them. Then I turn them upside down, one by one, and I pour them into the ocean.

He won't speak to me at all now.

In the morning I see a speck appear on the horizon, a black spot the size of an insect.

The point of blackness, which at first appears to be nothing more than a gnat, keeps coming closer, heading directly toward the island, and I tell myself that it must be a figment of my imagination. But after two minutes it assumes the form of a plane to such perfection that

I need a moment to recognize what it is. It is an ideal plane: silvery blue, it winks at me with flashes of sun-struck metal like a plane in a vision. At first I take off my scarf and gesticulate furiously, but as the plane appears to lose altitude, I begin to relax and wave to it calmly, welcoming it ashore. Everything about this plane conveys purpose and assurance, as if it had been designed solely to rescue us. I find the promise of its shape more beautiful than anything I have ever seen, but strangely lost to me, although I don't understand why until it comes closer and I am able to determine that despite my wish it is not coming toward the island at all. It looked as if it were heading directly at me, but as I watch it grow larger I see it pass overhead, high above, too far to see me as I desperately shake my scarf. It circles once — for an instant I imagine that it is heading toward the water and I think I can make out black pontoons for landing — and then it makes a wide turn, points back toward the mysterious place from whence it has come, and flies away. It hasn't seen me at all.

* * *

I don't feel despair when this happens. I don't feel disappointment or rage when the plane disappears, I feel only a bleak contempt for myself. I am fallen, earthbound, undeserving. What moves me is that the plane makes such a lovely sight, that it negotiates the sky with so much grace that it seems to exist in an atmosphere above reality. It's so beautiful it takes my breath away.

We couldn't have foreseen what would happen to us as a result of witnessing our own abandonment. It seemed impossible that the plane hadn't seen us, but equally impossible that it had and then just flew away. We never understood the meaning of the plane. It abandoned us. It was too terrible to believe, that our only hope, our one salvation, that the messenger we had been waiting for, the protection we had expected, was out there, it existed, but not for us. So at first we did not lose hope. We did not even worry. But gradually, in the hours and days to come, our hope abandoned us too, and all that was left was the memory of that plane. Like children, we adored the plane that abandoned us. We sat on the beach for a long time, waiting, cultivating our separate vivid images of the plane. We loved the plane even more after it left us, as if that might bring it back.

Seven

We didn't speak to each other for a long time. We were angry and we blamed our anger on each other. There were no more planes, no ships on the horizon. At first we kept track of the dates, counting the days, and then we stopped doing even that.

It lasted a long time, and then finally we couldn't be angry anymore. We abandoned hope, then worry, and then even our anger. It was easy: we never tried to do it, we just did, finally, because we had no choice.

We named the island Heaven, as a kind of joke, and we set about making it home. Noonan built himself a bungalow on the eastern end of the island. It was a shack with a veranda and a hammock made from a fuel cover. I built myself a lean-to by the lagoon, because the nights were cooler there, and the air was tinged with the scent of oleander. We set up a communication system using smoke signals and chimes fashioned from seashells. He would invite me over to his place for dinner, which he still prepared. He considered himself a chef. On a typical evening, he would collect fish from the inlet on the southern end of the island, small fish that swam so lazily they seemed to pause in the center of his palms and let themselves be scooped up by the dozens. Then he picked fruits and berries and made a salad which looked poisonous but was in fact delicious. He stole petals from the flowers and boiled water and herbs for a medicinal-tasting tea. Even if he had had the resources to cook the richest sauces, he would have preferred making do with the island vegetation because he liked the challenge of living by his wits.

His one luxury is simple: a mildly narcotic root he has discovered and which he smokes in a long, irregular pipe that he has fashioned out of tortoiseshell. I say *his* luxury, but the truth is I liked to smoke from it too. He used to smoke after dinner, and I would usually join him, but not until he cajoled me, out of habit, so I could have the pleasure of declining and then giving in. When we smoke I have visions of past flights: I feel my Electra, its vibrations, I see the landscape change below. Other times I imagine the outside world, what's happening to the world without me.

At that time, the time of Heaven, of the island, of our splendid isolation, Noonan has occasional fits of jealousy. He knows nothing of my visions, of my midnight flights. But I can see he's observing me, he suspects something. He knows her, his only friend, and there's a new remoteness about her, a separateness, that unnerves him, makes him jealous. She's distracted, absentminded, her expression has lost some of its openness. She's alert, but only to herself, to some inner fixation, and she's become an observer too, of herself, of their abandonment. It's as if she were a spectator to everything, even the secret dramas taking place in her own mind. What they are, he can't know. He has his own terrors, but he's consumed by hers, by wondering about her, being jealous of whatever it is that's taking her away from him. He has fits of jealousy in which he accuses her of all kinds of things: of purposely misleading him to this godforsaken nowhere, of wanting to kill them both, of being crazy. He's not angry, he's just trying to get her attention. He says he can see in her eyes that this was her plan all along, to bring him down with her. But when she doesn't defend herself, he starts to cry. What can he do, he's helpless without her.

He asks me what I'm thinking about, what I'm scheming. I can't tell him, can't put into words that all I think about is my plane, my lost Electra, lost but still here, tormenting me. At night she gleams with a divine, alien majesty. On the beach, when the water washes underneath her, she is a barge of beaten silver. All my anguish is bound up in the plane, although even in this state I know that doesn't make any sense. But it's all I have, my Electra, my dreams, my secret flights, my visions of escape. I don't want him to know about it. It's too private. I need something for myself. His voice lowers, he's confidential, trying to gain my trust, he wants to help me, but more than that he wants to know and I hate that, I hate that he wants to know, to take all of me, to leave me with nothing. Once, he hits me. He's so frustrated that he hits me. Anything to bring me back. He hits me hard, he's still strong. But I'm not afraid of him, I know he's the one afraid of me, and so it ends, the violence ends itself, calms us down, and it's over. He wants me to have forgotten everything that came before this, for me to be here, now, entirely.

I say to him, How could I be anywhere else? Where could I go? I'm stranded on a desert island.

We bicker constantly, for no good reason except to remind ourselves that we're alive. We fight about anything. I'm bossy and he's stubborn. Sometimes, when things get awful, we fight without words. This way we can both appear hurt.

We share a talent for pointless argument. When we feel like talking, we drag out a debate, picking over every turn of phrase, every insult. You would think that we would have no time for this sort of thing. After all, we're struggling to survive. But in fact we have all the time in the world, and we haven't yet discovered how to fill it.

But they always make up by the end of dinner, over music. Noonan will take out his harmonica and she'll sing. They sing ballads and ditties and advertising jingles, anything they can remember. Their favorite songs are "Home on the Range," "Good Ship Lollipop," and "Streets of Laredo." She has a wavering, delicate voice, but she can carry a tune, and the harmonica gives her courage and helps her along. The reedy sounds of her thin singing and the mournful jauntiness of Noonan's harmonica hang in the air long after they have put out the fire. The music keeps him sane when he is awake and the memory of it fends off bad dreams when he sleeps. In dreams the truth might be revealed to them, that they are each alone with their teasing glimmers and phantasms.

It takes us all evening to make dinner. We drag it out, like the bickering. Actually, it takes all day. From the first light of dawn we are concerning ourselves with dinner, with food, with survival. We check the water collection tanks. Depending on the precipitation and the dew, we shake off the leaves. By now Noonan's rigged up a permanent device for extracting fresh water from salt. It works slowly, but we treasure every drop.

Then we check on the crabs — we've built a coop and we're fattening them up — and the fish colony we've created. Sometimes Noonan works on the boat he's building, and I collect fruit, or work on my lean-to. Sometimes I write in my pilot's log. We do what we have to to make the days fly.

He sets out every afternoon to catch fish for dinner, and sometimes she comes along, the two of them chatting about odd subjects as they make their way along the reef flat to the inlet. If she doesn't come, he has a smoke by himself, and signals to her when he's ready to start preparing dinner.

Then she will appear from the depths of the jungle, branches tangled in her wide-brimmed hat woven from dried leaves, carrying kindling for their fire. She has a flair for engineering, and so her arrangements of wood are always complex structures, and the more she misses flying the more elaborate they become. She builds replicas of the Hoover Dam, the Eiffel Tower, and then, when she is at her most despairing, a scale model of the Brooklyn Bridge. This last one is too long and delicate to be efficient, and it possesses a sublime weightlessness that prevents Noonan from being able to light it. She exasperates him with her lofty creations.

She feels that he uses too much sea salt in his cooking. She asks him casually, when she sees him measure out a handful, whether he is planning to put all of that in. Sometimes her criticisms are more direct, and usually his responses are bitingly defensive. But she has to admit that he's an excellent cook. She's too competitive to come right out and say it. Instead she lets the pressure of his expertise inspire her to create ever more inventive desserts. The last course has become her domain. They don't have a wide variety of ingredients to choose from, and so she makes just about everything out of coconut.

How do you want your coconut tonight? she asks.

Medium rare, he says.

Hmm, an aristocrat.

It smells delicious, the coconut frying up over the fire, sweet and sugary, sizzling in its juices.

When you think of life on a desert island, you get pictures in your mind of cannibals and pirates, of desolation and thirst. But at first it wasn't at all like that for us. It really wasn't bad. We dined on fresh fish and sea vegetables under a canopy of stars. I would throw another piece of coconut on the fire and Noonan would take up his harmonica. Anyone else stranded on a desert island would probably have wanted to die, but for him the nights had never been more beautiful, the wind more gentle, the sea more calm. I missed my Electra, I missed it desperately, but I had to agree, we were lucky, in a way.

After dinner, he plays a composition he's written for me. He calls it "Perhapsody in Blue."

I remember that at around this time he returned to the navigator's cabin of the Electra, which he had been studiously avoiding. He dusted off the navigational charts, which had rolled themselves up into gigantic cylinders, and the radio, which hung out of the dashboard by a wire. He brought them back to his shack. There he set about figuring out where we had landed, charting a course, and attempting to make contact with passing ships. There was only a tiny amount of gas left, but it was enough to let us dream. I said why don't we take her for a spin around the block. But in his enthusiasm Noonan convinced himself that we could reach Australia, or New Zealand.

After dinner, I go to the lagoon. He comes with me. There's a raft that I built, I like to lie there in the darkness, where my thoughts are more intense because they seem to be taking place on board a dock that has broken off and floated out to sea. But Noonan prefers the water itself. The stars tilt and wobble on the surface when we enter. It rolls in folds like the back of a dog's neck. And as we circle each other, our feet skimming the murky bottom, our legs beat languidly and the water slips through our fingers in endless sheets of silk. The lagoon isn't large, but it's enormous in the night, like a lake on the surface of the moon.

But I won't let him sleep in my lean-to. I won't let him spend the night. I leave him after we swim and I go to my plane. My once magnificent Electra.

Eight

Edwin Earhart. My father — of humble origins, and later, a ne'er-do-well. He'd been poor and had worked for his education. He had tutored more-privileged students at law school, where one of his laziest but kindest pupils had been Mark Otis. Mark had brought Edwin home for his sister's sixteenth-birthday party, and there, in the wood-paneled dining room of the house on the hill, he and Amy Otis had fallen in love. Years later, when he wandered the business districts of the cities he lived in, intoxicated and abandoned by all desire to persevere, the sight of well-dressed people would remind Edwin of the crystal chandelier that dangled over the Otises' dining room like a gaudy earring, and the limpid, watery sparkle it cast across the table that first night he came to visit, sending rainbow shards through the long-stemmed glasses and patterning the plates with mad diagrams. Dancing flames from the fireplace made faces in the windows. Mutton and puddings and warm bread were handled like fragile cargo by a regiment of silent maids. Mesmerized by the opulence and order, Edwin had a glint in his eye that gave him a deceptive air of success, and the wine he drank with dinner improved his already good looks. Delicate Amy, her father's favorite, my mother, looked across the table at him adoringly.

I was bolder than my mother would have liked: I insisted on running around in my bloomers. But my pluck and mettle delighted my father, an apprehensive man with a cowardly nature who liked to tinker with mechanical things and harbored delusions of intrepidity himself. He taught me how to take apart clocks and bicycles, and later, with only a few illicit lessons in a motorcar, he taught me to drive like a professional.

In 1903, my father attempted to secure a patent for an invention he'd been working on for years. It was a holder for signal flags at the rear of railway cars, and he believed it to be revolutionary. He worked on it whenever he could, and when he was distracted or nervous he would excuse his behavior by saying, It's the invention, Meelie, it never leaves me. He kept it a secret, but he managed to convince his daughter that it was the key to their future happiness. Finally, after much arguing with his wife, he went off to Washington, D.C., financing the trip with money that the family had saved to pay off debts and taxes. He was gone for five days — he sent a postcard home with a picture of the White House and a message that arrived too blurred with rain or tears for us to read. As luck would have it, someone from Colorado had filed a patent on the same invention two years before.

When she thinks of her father now, she sees him at the end of the day. That's his time of day, twilight, or just before. The late afternoon, when the sun is setting, when it feels sad and beautiful, like the last day. When the sadness is too unbearable to think about, and this makes you strangely cheerful.

Sam Chapman. He was my first real

beau. He was a boarder in my parents' house in California. He was an engineer, a college graduate from back East, with a dimpled, charming, carefree face and sloped, solid shoulders. One night, not long after we first met, he told me his life story on the darkened porch, as the sun set over the empty street, the smell of the desert blowing in on a dry wind. It wasn't anything special. It was an American life, with a pleasant childhood, a family, an accident, a stint in the war. It was actually fairly dull. But no man had ever opened up to me that way, it was my first taste of intimacy. That night, I felt a ribbon of warmth work its way up the back of my neck, and later I noticed in the mirror that my cheeks were flushed fuchsia. I had trouble going to the bathroom: I was too excited to pee.

Sam escorted me to movies, and to amusement parks, and once we held hands at a Wobbly meeting, where, fired by the fury of the workers of the world, we almost kissed in public, but suddenly the hall was flooded with police. There were people in those days who believed the world could be a better place. Sam was one of them, but like many people who want the world to be better, he didn't really like change. Instead, he wanted the world to change around him, while he kept his basically old-fashioned views.

Once I started flying seriously, he let me know what he really thought of women pilots, and so our time together became strained. I attempted to take him up in a plane before I had my license, but when we crashed on the beach I was so unperturbed that he called me a selfish menace.

As the shy skinny girl he first met grows into a woman, Sam begins to consider the possibility that their future together is not something to be taken for granted, and so he drives into downtown Los Angeles, withdraws his savings from the Western Bank, and purchases a diamond ring, all during the course of his lunch hour. Walking with her on the beach the next day, the light softly tangled in her blowing hair, her face seen very close and clearly for a moment like a shell suddenly uncovered by the tide, he feels that he is loving her for the first time, and his heart stops with dread when he hears her voice. It reaches him as if it were spoken from inside him.

Oh, Sam, she says, I'm so flattered.

He looks out at the water when she says this. He sees two sailboats moving at opposite ends of the ocean.

What does that mean, flattered? he says to the water.

It means that I'm honored you would think of asking me.

It means no, that's what it means.

Years later, when she tells him before she tells anyone else that she is flying across the Atlantic, she recognizes the pained expression, the pinched eyes, the tightened mouth, from that day on the beach. She wants to laugh and pretend that he's only pouting. Before she leaves, she asks him to tell her mother and sister for her as soon as she's taken off. She gives him two letters to give to them. In the letters she writes that she knows what she's doing. She accepts the hazards. She has to go.

He watches her lips promise to send him a postcard from somewhere. Waving goodbye, he says to himself that that is her style: intimately heartless. He can tell by the way she smiles at him, that she has no idea how unhappy he is.

The temperature exploded. There is no other way to describe it. The heat rose steadily all day, but there was a breeze in the morning and so we didn't notice the change at first. The jungle was as quiet as on any other morning. The birds were by the lagoon. But what we did not know was that they were drinking the water, getting ready for the heat. They had a way of knowing what was coming up, a way that eluded us. They congregated around the lagoon in strange formations, like supplicants of some exotic religion.

On the first day of the heat wave, I hear the birds talking to one another around the edge of the water. They have been at the lagoon since the earliest light of dawn. They are gathering force. The vicinity of the lagoon is exceptionally buggy. The insects also are preparing for the heat.

When I see Noonan for the first time that morning, he's taken off his shirt, like a soldier stripped for combat.

A bolt of lightning that announces the

heat wave strikes about a mile out to sea. We catch sight of it as we emerge from the jungle onto the beach. It sizzles in the distance, a sinister line of yellow in the sky, and it leaves a dark impression in its afterglow. I see the bright flash for a few more seconds, hanging in the bright white sky. By the time it has faded completely from my vision, there is such a noticeable change in the weather, which had been hot but bearable a minute before, that Noonan has wrapped his shirt in a turban around his head, Arabian style. Heat seems to rise around us on all sides, and over the beach we see the air ripple in waves, as if the sand had turned to flames. The sky is cloudless. In the sky we see only the rays of the sun beating down on the sand and reflecting back.

The heat will take over the island. It will keep up all day and all night for several weeks. The sun beats down, the air is still, the deafening hum goes on. The things that will happen could only have happened during a heat wave. Everything becomes quite unreal and it seems as though there is no future. It is impossible to think about the future during the heat wave. All during the heat wave we have the feeling, even in the darkness, that we need to escape from the sun.

That first afternoon we stay around the lagoon. All of the animals gravitate there. There's a haze of insects. The birds step in and out of the water, delicately, like ladies. In the jungle it's as if someone lit a match under every leaf. It shimmers with heat. Huge tropical rats with long silken tails run in circles, made crazy by the heat. Giant crabs scurry up the vines. Eventually, the lagoon grows shallow and its waters stagnate into a cesspool on top of which winged bugs float belly up, their tiny legs shriveled in morbid curlicues. At night it will become necessary to sleep under the cloth fuel covers to protect ourselves from the mosquitoes, and then being alive seems worse than death. To the heat and the mosquitoes there will be added the stench of dead marine life that the tide leaves behind on the reef.

After a while she gives up sleep and

spends the nights roaming the beach, swatting away insects with her silk scarf.

The water in our tanks dried up and the dew on the leaves was whisked away by the sun. Our lips cracked and our tongues turned white. We drank what coconut milk we could, but it gave us grinding stomachaches. We sucked on the jungle leaves. We felt a mortal thirst; it throbbed in our chests and then it hurt. Nevertheless, each time our spirits sank, something would happen to renew our hope. Sometimes it was just a sunset. It was a beautiful sunset. It was the finest sunset of the heat wave, and the temperature seemed to intensify the colors. Or maybe our delirium did.

From the meager shade of the palms, I watch the fruit-punch colors of the sun reflect off the burnished metal of the Electra. It glistens like a mirage on the sand. It's on fire, blazing. It reminds me of a sunset seen from a fire escape in New York City, the red sky coming down like a curtain over the purple Palisades. But the heat here doesn't end, it seems incapable of ending. We play twenty questions. We talk to keep ourselves sane.

Somewhere, it's raining, I say to Noonan.

I know, he says. Try not to think about it.

For long stretches of time we're completely silent. Long after sunset we're still sitting there, on the sand. I recognize the terror of the quiet, the silence of flying. Everything is moving, but everything is still.

In the middle of the night I woke up. I sat in the Electra and tried to console myself. I was so tired that I rested my head on the wheel and prepared to fall asleep and die. That was when I saw G.P., sitting next to me in the cockpit, smoking a cigar. I hadn't thought about my husband for a long time. I had thought about a lot of figures from my past, but I had not thought about G.P. since the day the plane abandoned us, and I had assumed he'd given me up for dead. But now, as soon as I closed my eyes, he appeared to me, sitting next to me, smoking, first holding his cigar between his fingers, then puffing on it, then holding a telephone in his lap and handing me the receiver.

At first, it was a dream. G.P. would appear to me in my sleep, always next to me, smoking that cigar. He spoke to me, and I said something back. I couldn't hear what I was asking and I didn't understand what he answered, but I knew that we were talking in the cockpit of the Electra and then suddenly there was the shock of the fall, the fatal fall, and I woke up with a start.

It was still dark. I had long ago given up trying to see a plane on the horizon, but shortly before dawn a shimmering light seemed to rise up from the water and I looked out to sea. That was when I saw G.P. standing a few feet away from me on the beach, dressed in his familiar gray felt fedora and gray suit, his silk tie fluttering in the wind.

He stood there, waiting, for a long time, and then I got out of the plane and climbed down from the wing.

Hello, G.P., I said.

It's so damn hot here, he said.

If this had been a dream, or a hallucination, I might have forgotten it. But I was awake, I was hungry and thirsty,

I could hear the shattering surf.

Why didn't you take the trailing wire for the radio? he asked me.

Because it was too long, it was a nuisance, I answered.

Why didn't you put a signal on Howland Island? he said.

Because you wouldn't let me. I raised my voice.

It seemed ridiculous that he was berating me now, and I wished he were only an apparition.

He said nothing. Then he lit himself a cigar and took a few puffs. The flame from his match illuminated his silver cuff link and cast a reddish glow, for an instant, over his face. He blew out the match and stared out into the darkness. Then, holding the lit cigar in his thick fingers, he pointed out to the ocean. I followed his direction with my gaze, and there they were: the crystalline lights of the Manhattan skyline, twinkling in the distance. For a long time I looked at the lights of the city, without happiness, without despair either, as if I were coming in for a landing after an ordinary, everyday flight.

The lights flit and sparkle. I ask G.P.

if he will walk with me to the end of the beach so that I can get a better look at the city. But he isn't there. I'm standing on the beach, and as the sun comes up, the lights of Manhattan turn into early-morning stars. Another day of the heat wave dawns.

The water looks empty. Suddenly a fin slices through the surface. Then another, and another. They are circling, close together. They circle for several minutes, and then come two more and then three others, which are racing to join in. You can sense that they are coming in for a kill, and all of a sudden a fish leaps out of the water, freely, in a perfect arc. Then there is a mad rush toward the center, and then a flowering of red. It all happens very quickly. One fish floats up to the surface, its head torn off, and spins quietly.

I am exhausted with desire for my plane.

I crawl into the cockpit, in the heat of the day. My hands leave dark, wet palm prints on everything I touch. I want to take my Electra for another ride, I want to wheel above the clouds, to soar above this weather. I want to find weather that will cheer me up. I want to drink from the rain that rains beyond the sun. I consider actually starting the engine, using what little fuel we have left, and diving over the sun. I wish I could tell you what stops me, but I can't. I'm still hoping, hope against hope.

I haven't forgotten G.P. I haven't forgotten the man with the hat. And I'm still on the island. It's where I live, the only place I know how to exist. It's in my plane, my Electra, burning on the beach, that I'll write my story, my book. It's the place where, later on, I'll lift my way into the future. In my plane, all alone, I'm at work on the extraordinary preparations for my future. But during the heat wave I don't know that yet. During the heat wave it's impossible to think about the future.

I don't know what happened to G.P. I don't even know when he died. I assume he remarried, he always had to have a wife. It must have been a long time before he could fly. I wonder if he ever flew again. Actually, as I remember, he never really liked to fly.

Nine

Let me tell you what happened next, what it was like. It was like the end of the world.

We hid in the Electra for shelter. The rain drummed down on the beaten metal and the wind whistled in through the loosening screws. The navigator's cabin still housed some of our charts — which now lay strewn on the floor, flattened by footsteps or curled up in giant cylinders — and the illuminated table, Noonan's shoes, and his instruments. Through the specially installed windows we could see the palms bending in the storm, curving and tossing and throwing their hair in a tempestuous dance against death.

But before all this, there was the dry storm. The storm between the heat wave and the rain.

The heat wave lasted for several

weeks, at the end of which we were strangers. We had changed so much, the heat had taken so much, we were strangers to ourselves. We spent our time together, but we barely spoke anymore. What was there to say? We were desiccated, blistered. Noonan had done everything he could: he'd built us shelter, he'd perfected his device for extracting water, he'd made us a little boat. But still the sun was too much for us. One day, he went out in his boat, and by the time he came back he was bleeding from the heat. He'd covered himself, but the sun had burned through his protection, and he was so cooked that his skin peeled and then bled.

It was at night that the electrical storm ignited. We hadn't seen lightning for a long time, just sun, or haze, but now a bolt of lightning struck out at sea and crackled in the air, suspended for so long that it lit up the entire island. It was like being on a film set, with the giant lights. The bolt of lightning illuminated the sky. It made the night day. All of the color was washed out, but the light was there, deadly, supernatural. There was no rain, just electricity. The electricity was palpable in the air. The atmosphere tingled. The animals were terrified, but fascinated. They pricked up their ears. At first it felt exciting, and fresh. But it went on for a long time this way, the lightning crashing through the night, ferocious, blinding. Everything was waiting for the rain to come, but it didn't. We were being teased. We'd waited so long you'd have thought we could have waited another night, but it was excruciating. The air felt menacing and alive. I didn't know that you could expect that from nature, such manipulation, such deep anger.

It was a gray morning, the next morning, the morning the storm began. A Friday, I think it was. We had stopped counting the days. But then I started again, picking up where we had left off. It may not have been Friday anywhere else, but it was Friday on our island.

He told me to hide in the Electra. He'd been around the world on ships, he knew what he was talking about, but I challenged him. I didn't believe him. I said it seemed that the Electra would be a dangerous place to go, that it might attract the lightning. He said the lightning was over, we'd seen the last of it.

And then he looked at me. No, he said. Actually, you're right. I thought I would try to get us killed.

Night fell suddenly, in the middle of the day. Just as the first storm brought the daylight to the darkness, this one turned the sun black. First the clouds massed, then they turned purple, bruising before our eyes, and then a wind came down on a thousand horses and threatened to annihilate the island. It was one of those storms that was like a disease. When you are sick you can't remember being well. During the storm it seemed as if there had never been any other weather, anything but storm.

We watched the storm from the Electra. Or, I watched it. Noonan smoked his pipe, he smoked so that the entire plane was filled with ribbons and then sheets of his smoke. He sat slumped in a corner, not caring about the storm, or caring so much that he couldn't watch it. During the heat wave, he had thought about dying, but now here he was, still alive. He was alive and the storm was bringing us water, and fish, and, if not a reason to live, at least the possibility. But he was past possibilities.

I think it was then, during the storm, while we were waiting, that he finally understood what had happened to us.

In the morning the beach was transformed into a Sunday boardwalk, with coconuts and orchid petals and anemones and fish strewn about the sand like the remnants of a Saturday night.

She spends the morning watching the birds pick at the debris, she watches them fight over fish and pass over urchins, and she does not realize for quite some time that Noonan is among them, squawking and clucking and bickering. She sees him when he is already deeply engaged in conversation with a bird of paradise, gesticulating madly, with his radio in one hand and a piece of fish in his mouth. She calls out to him, but he doesn't respond, and she sees him walk away from her, lost in argument with a bird, and then soon afterward she sees him round the bend of the beach and disappear from her sight.

* * *

Then she feels completely alone.

Three days later, on an exquisitely clear night, she found herself in the traditional state of a stranded islander, with a melancholy composed of memories and regrets, and too much time on her hands. Noonan had survived the storm with a poetic stoicism, taking their exile to its purest extreme. He appeared that night wearing flowers in his hair, he danced alone on the sand in the transparent moonlight, and before daybreak she decided that he was lost to her and to the rest of the world forever. Heartbroken with grief, she had gone to sit in the cockpit, where his singing couldn't reach her, and she put on her goggles and her skullcap in an effort to overcome the desire to join him in his madness. It was a time of torment, which ended at dawn when she sighted the shore of her island through the broken windshield of her plane, and she decided once and for all that she had taken this journey in order to escape the madness of the world, that she didn't give a damn if she was alone, she wouldn't go crazy, and that she would live the rest of her long and brilliant life on this wild and desolate island.

It took her several days to turn her lean-to into a house, and then she felt she was home again. From the moment she hung a mirror over the makeshift mantelpiece and saw her reflection in the piece of aluminum that she had broken off from the navigator's table, she felt that life was good again. She was still recognizable to herself as herself, but she had a new expression. She could see in the atmosphere around her eyes that she had lived through something tremendous, in the way that people who have survived a traumatic experience or accident always look palpably changed. Her skin was brown, not just freckled, for the first time in her life. But she was so eager to finish fixing up her new house that she didn't have the time to examine her features. She stuffed a bed with dried leaves and made a pillow out of her silk shirt. She fashioned a table and chair out of branches and twine. One day, when she was bored, she carved herself a set of utensils in the same pattern she'd eaten from at her grandmother Otis's house.

Before she put the last touches on the place she performed a symbolic act: she threw her silver compact into the ocean, and followed it with her eyes as it floated over the sharks, dipped between the waves, and disappeared into the Pacific. She was sure she would never need it again. There would be no more photographers.

The lagoon was calm the first morning she woke up in her new home. Above a bluish mist she saw the tops of the trees, emerald in the first light of day, and she saw the coconuts hanging in testicular arrangements, and orienting herself by the clusters of fruit, she located a nest of two birds, where she supposed the cooing lovers were still engaged, their beaks nestling into each other's breasts. The idea broke her heart, but she did nothing to avoid it. For the first time, she took pleasure in her pain. The sun was getting hot as the mist lifted off the lagoon, where the countless aromas of opening flowers and decomposing mulch at the bottom of the water congealed into one pungent, unhuman smell. The screech of birds had begun, and gangs of frogs in water up to their necks snatched butterflies from floating leaves. She fried herself a banana over her metal stove. She had taken another piece of Noonan's table and turned it into an oven, and from that moment on she was no longer bothered by the hothouse environment of her new home but was only aware of the sweet scent of sizzling fruit.

She does not concern herself with being rescued. Her only interest seems to be in dismantling the Electra to furnish her house and in the meticulous record of her experiences, which she continues to write, lying in her hammock, in her pilot's logbook. She does not try to talk sense into Noonan, or to save him. She establishes her own daily routine, and sometimes she and Noonan run into each other while they are fishing at dusk amidst the sharks, or getting water at dawn from the collection tanks, but she does not wait for him in the jungle or go to his end of the island at night. She cannot even allow herself to dream of that.

Sometimes she goes for walks on the

beach, her dark shadow trailing behind her like the train of a long black dress.

She realizes that she is alone on the island, in spirit at least, and she takes it for granted that it will remain that way, if not forever, for many years to come. This certainty fills her with her first hope of accepting her circumstances. It was during this time that she let her hair grow again, weaving it into the long, thick braid that she would keep for the rest of her life.

She develops habits that seem incredible in someone like herself, focused and driven and ambitious. She stops waking at dawn and sleeps until noon. She forgets to bathe for days. She lets animals roam her lean-to, and sometimes she falls asleep with a monkey by her feet and a bird perched on her stomach. She walks the beaches in search of truths that had never troubled her in their absence: she thinks about death and miracles and solitude. These were the days when she became reacquainted with herself, without hoping for anything except the satisfaction of knowing that she had explored an unknown sensation or feeling. This was her only object, and in its pursuit she discovered that she knew only a small portion of the vast landscape that was her soul. It was as if what she had considered to be her self all these years was only a magnified detail of an enormous painting whose entire composition and narrative she had never before known existed, let alone seen. And in this way she began to view the universe differently.

The sky, however wide and smeared with thick, painterly clouds, now seems to her only one square inch of an infinite fresco of the world.

She thinks about her past, her family. She remembers that it was her father who first took her to see an air show.

By the time we moved to Los Angeles, my father was a broken man. He spent his luxuriously empty days wandering the streets like an old cowboy. My mother was already sick, and he was in the habit of attending circuses and flea markets. He initiated me into the secrets of his favorite pastime. The Winter Air Tournament was held on Christmas Day. The show included races, aerobatics, and wing walking, all performed by handsome young men who wandered the grounds with their leather jackets unbuttoned and their sweaty hair plastered to their brows in dark scars. I was still demure enough to attend an event such as this wearing a strand of my grandmother's heirloom pearls and a pair of embroidered gloves.

Now, when she tries to remember her first excursion in an airplane, she can't distinguish it from the heavenly beauty of California in 1921. It was a few months after the air show. The spring came suddenly: the rains stopped, the days grew noticeably longer, and the afternoon light felt powdery, as if it might blow away. She doesn't remember that maiden voyage, but she remembers walking across the airfield when she stepped out of the plane. Strong, fresh skirts of breeze brushed against her face and body as she walked across the landing strip. Strands of her long, honey-blond hair swept into her line of sight. She looked out past the hangars, over a field of tall, dry grass, and in the buttery light, with the wind grazing past her, she thought she could see forever. She had the sensation of seeing a length of time stretch out in front of her, endlessly, effortlessly, on an invisible wing. She felt as though an experience she had always anticipated were about to take place, as if a tender, unearthly feeling were finally going to reveal its secret to her. The vision came so vividly that she imagined her father — he had come to watch her flight — had seen it too. But when she turned around, her hair blowing now in the opposite direction, he was looking down, stubbing a cigarette out with his foot, smiling over something with one of the airfield mechanics.

Love is so transparent that if you are unprepared for it you will see right through it and not notice it.

One night, Noonan took refuge in her house because his living area had been infested with rats. It was he who took control of the situation and made up a blanket for himself on the floor under the pretext that he couldn't stand the scrambling of the rats at his place. In this situation it seemed obvious to her that he should sleep at the far end of the lean-to, behind the little stove. But he had already made the decision for both of them. He spread his blanket down beside the hammock in which she had been writing frantically in her pilot's log, not knowing how to behave in the face of his presumed madness, and he began to speak to her about the changes on his end of the island, in the meantime removing his threadbare trousers and his glasses, both of which he folded carefully and placed gingerly at the foot of his new bed. He took the garland of flowers that he always wore now from around his neck and hung it from the mirror, he removed the necklaces woven from roots and placed them on the table beside the dictionary of pidgin English, with one graceful gesture he slipped off his bracelets carved from coral, his shark's-tooth earring, and his monkey-hair anklet, and he spread everything out around the lean-to until the room was decorated with the accoutrements of his dementia. He did it all with so much piety, and with such meaningful pauses, that each of his removals seemed sacred.

She tried to help him untie the feathers from his hair, but he took her fingers and kissed them and put them in his mouth, all the while working on the feathers himself, until they were strewn around him like the colorful remnants of a pillow fight among concubines in a harem.

His body is lean but still strong, and his skin is surprisingly soft, worn smooth by the salt and sand, like a stone. He's gentle with her, and when he looks at her he smiles, and then his smile, not the smile of the gambler but the smile of the gentleman, the wild gentleman, his smile turns to tears.

She's afraid of him at first, but then she realizes that like herself, he too has changed. They are still the pilot and the navigator, but they've forgotten their parts, their professions. They don't have names, or memories, or words.

I want to tell you everything without saying anything, he says. And she agrees. And they do that, from now on, they tell each other everything.

* * *

That night, he stopped talking to the animals, although he continued to wear the feathers and the bracelets and the earring, and he began to share his body with her whenever she asked for it. He built himself a cabin on the more gentle, western end of the island, with a terrace that overlooked the sea and where the surf would sing itself to sleep on velvet winds. This was his hideaway, as he called it, where he would receive his visitor at any hour of the day or night, without asking questions or expecting anything in return because in his opinion it was the least he could do for the woman who had saved his life. Sometimes he would accept a gift from her, a poem or some fried banana, but he never liked to feel that they were involved in any kind of barter. Only once did he refuse her, when he was feeling sick from eating too many handfuls of fish eggs, but otherwise he never turned her down, even if he wasn't in the mood.

Ten

He visits me at night in my house by the lagoon. We are lovers. We love each other all night.

Sometimes he comes to me in the middle of the night, and we drench ourselves in the slick and perfumed waters of the lagoon, making folds in the wetness as if we are moving through a timeless and moonlit cave of space.

After so much loneliness, so long, so alone, the sound of another person's voice or just their breathing is a feeling unto itself. It's a deep joy in the body, like having water run through you. The sound of his breathing keeps me asleep for hours.

With all his experience, he tries to teach her the tricks he has performed or seen performed on others, but the lessons are unnecessary. She isn't looking for drama, she just wants to be satisfied. The truth is that she was bored by the limited coupling she had with her husband and she enjoys the unencumbered sex with Noonan, but in both cases she takes it lightly. She thinks of it like eating: sometimes she has a good meal, sometimes she has a bad one, but usually she's just hungry and she eats. For a long time Noonan lives under the delusion that because she seems untheatrical in bed she is frightened or uncomfortable. But little by little he comes to understand that she can enjoy herself without telling him about it. In this way he comes to trust her. And he believes that they will be able to please themselves forever because they don't protect each other from their selfishness.

They weren't expecting or forcing themselves to be in love. He had given her the gift of an unconventional free-dom, which she deemed more precious than love.

It happens at night, by the lagoon on the desert island. Every night the great heroine gives herself to the navigator, and every night he gives himself back.

The rest of the world will never give up on them, will never stop looking for them. But there they are, alive. They're living for each other now.

During the day she looks at the horizon, suspiciously. She doesn't say anything about it to Noonan. She goes on loving him, receiving him at night. She watches for him and waits. Neither of them will break their unspoken rule. Neither of them will talk about the future. But she has premonitions. She has nightmares.

With love come the deepest fears of dying.

At night, under the moon, the cool slippery water, the wet salty bodies, the famous silk scarf, and there they go, into an atmosphere of their own, where they splash each other, sing songs to each other, please each other, slowly, with all the time in the world, then on the raft, floating like a leaf on the water, then to the bed stuffed with feathers and leaves, their bodies leaving dark wet impressions behind them, and they'll be there all night, with the Electra on the beach watching over their island in the darkness, unafraid for themselves as long as they are together, oblivious to the world they have left behind, reminded of it only in their dreams.

It was late, almost morning, when he first saw the silver speck on the horizon, lit by the moon. She was asleep. Then dawn came, played tricks with his eyes. Then, with the sun, it flashed in and out of sight. He doesn't dare wake her. But she will wake up. Later, by the time the birds have taken their midday naps, she will have made him so happy he will have forgotten all about the silver speck on the horizon.

Eleven

On the occasion of their first anniversary on the island, they prepared a celebration for themselves, the climax of which was a gigantic shark the color of slate which turned on a spit over a roaring fire, some seven hours simmering in its own juices. Half the animals on the island gathered to express their wonderment. She and Noonan had spent the weeks beforehand plotting how to lure a shark into a trap of coconut and wire, and they were celebrating their catch as much as their anniversary. They had carried the beast from one end of the island to the other, and now they felt they knew it well enough to eat it. When they opened him up, they found a solid gold cigarette case in his stomach.

Lost in the aroma of sizzling sharkskin which gained pungency as the day wore on, she felt herself in agreement with the world, whose calm pulse could be felt over the din of the animals and the fire. Everything was perfect, or perfectly imperfect. The shark fell into the fire and its skin burned to a crisp. It was too rare. They ate very well. Noonan's fin soup was a success, but the birds got most of the meat.

After dinner he took out his harmonica and we made music, the way we had when we first landed on the island, familiar songs from our past, and radio hits that we remembered. We sang ballads and cowboy tunes, and advertising jingles, anything that we knew. There was a new sweetness to our singing, because the songs reminded us of a life we had lived a very long time ago, a life that we remembered but did not miss.

We sang long after the arrival of the last few stars, thrown about in their lunatic patterns, each with a color and shape of its own, suspended in the clear black sky.

We sang to the dark, mysterious ocean, whose silence reached us like a mystical vapor.

We shared a smoke from Noonan's tortoiseshell pipe.

Excited by the lingering smell of the shark and by the singing, hundreds of fireflies electrified the beach, like Christmas lights dangling around invisible trees.

An hour later we were lying in each other's arms, on the edge of the foaming sea, and we made love almost as an afterthought on the broad, damp carpet of sand. The night insects were out in full force, with nothing to stop them from devouring our unprotected limbs, the sand snaked its way into every conceivable crevice, and the hermit crabs scuttled through our tangled hair, which by now had grown so long it was remarkable that the rats hadn't already nested in it. We both wanted to keep going till sunrise, we had never felt such a cascade of passion, but we had to stop abruptly because Noonan was stung by the six-foot tentacle of a jellyfish. We hobbled our way back to the fire, which was by then a pile of ashes and shark's teeth, and we dragged ourselves inside the shack, where I fell asleep for thirteen hours. Noonan told me he stayed awake, he had a hard time not waking me, but instead he watched the breath flow in and out of my nostrils, with a concentration that he had not devoted to anything since he had tried to watch a flower grow when he was a child. When I woke up he was able to tell me all about my dreams.

Three days later, after a supper of the last of the shark fin soup, they went for a midnight swim in the lagoon, where they were both struck at the same moment with the realization that they had never been so happy. Implicit but unspoken in their epiphany was the understanding that they had never been happy before at all. Each of them had known pleasure, and triumph, and satisfaction, but they had never really tasted happiness. They said nothing of this to each other, not only because it wasn't necessary to say out loud, but also because to say it would have made them both inconsolably sad. Instead they performed tricks for each other in the water, and Amelia pretended to be a bareback rider like the women she had seen in circuses as a child. She stood high on a rock with her body three quarters exposed and she held out her arms in a soaring gesture as if she were floating in the air. She had flowers in her hair and the water dripped from her neck over her breasts and down her stomach. She looked like a statue come to life: part woman, part fountain, part tree.

That, along with so many other images of her captured in the course of their long association, will suddenly appear to him at the whim of fate, and disappear just as quickly when he sees her real face, lined and tan and intent on something. But the images, they live a life of their own in his mind, and he measures the passage of time less in terms of his own experience than in the changing expression of her form.

When she is old, gray-haired, he will love her for all of the seasons she contains.

One day, while she was napping, he went to catch fish in his favorite spot, a wild inlet where the coral reef teemed with tropical life, and he sat down to meditate before he worked. All at once, in the bright blue mirror of the sky, he caught a glimpse of an airplane barely visible on the horizon. It grew clearer. It developed before him as if it were a picture of a plane, coming to life in a chemical solution. It moved with a speed that he had not witnessed in so many months that it seemed supernatural, and it appeared to be heading directly toward the island. He watched it with a calm detachment at first, because he assumed it was a hallucination.

Holding his breath, he observed the machine at his leisure. He saw it grow large as if seen through time-lapse photography, and he saw it glide stealthily over the island, in wide circles, like a shark. From his solitary position he watched the plane as if he were watching an episode from his past or his future fly by, and he lingered, for more than an hour he lingered, unseen, escaping history. Then he caught six yellow fish for dinner and smoked a little on his pipe to pass the time until he saw the plane sweep around in one last arc and disappear into the slowly fading blue. It passed close enough above him so that he thought he could make out black pontoons for landing on the water.

It isn't until two hours later, over

dinner, that he tells her about the plane.

You know what, she says, I was right. You've been smoking too much of that stuff.

She is heading to check the water collection tanks, making her way through jungle still redolent of last night's rain, when she looks up through the canopy of leaves. She has to repress a trembling unlike anything she has ever experienced when she sees the image of her dreams and her night-mares crawling across the space of sky delineated by a cluster of shiny green leaves. It is very far away, but it is so dazzling, a glint of pure silver sliding like mercury through the blue, that it seems close enough for her to touch.

She thinks about many things when she sees the plane. She thinks that she's seeing things. She waits a long time for the vision to disappear. She splashes her face with water from the collection tank. But the plane is ada-mant, it doesn't go away, so she chooses to believe that it is more than a dream. She does not, however, fully accept its presence; it is too much of a shock for that. All at once she is cata-pulted into thoughts of rescue, and then to thoughts of capture.

It is impossible to tell from this dis-tance whether the plane is friend or foe, American or Japanese, or someone else. If it's an American plane, it would be waiting to see evidence of their presence before making a difficult landing. If it is Japanese, and since it is likely they have fallen into Japanese waters, it would be waiting for the same thing, and the appropriate time to pounce. They would not be treated kindly by the Japanese. They would not appreciate her presence: they would assume that she was a spy. Maybe they would feel the need to send her home, she is so famous, but maybe not: she is pre-sumed dead. No one would know if they captured her. She could be valuable. She could be brought into Saipan on an enemy barge, pulled slowly, stand-ing beside her Electra. She thinks about Noonan, what he would have to endure. She feels a fear spread like liquid through her body. She squints into the sky to see if the plane has come closer.

She considered the possibility that they were on the verge of being rescued. The mere idea stirred old desires. She thought about what used to be called home — the way she had when she first landed on the island, only this time her memories did not make her swoon with guilt and regret but instead made her tremble with fear. There was not much consolation. She looked up at the sky and the plane was still there. She started walking more quickly through the jungle.

As I walk back through the jungle to Noonan's end of the island, everything looks changed. I have never seen the trees before. I have never seen the birds before, nor the rats or the coconut crabs. It is all different. I feel as I once felt coming home from a crack-up. I was driving from the airfield through the familiar streets of the city, and everything was new. They were watering lawns and playing catch in the street, and I pulled the car up onto the side of the road and watched. It was strange. Then I went on, and the sound of the car seemed to be far away, and everything seemed to be coming from a long way off, and I could hear the sound of the motor as if it were the sound of a radio playing two blocks away. I had crashed badly. It's like that crossing the jungle.

In the jungle, the merciless heat. The great heroine leans against a tree, closes her eyes, lets the bugs sit on her shoulders, she's used to them now. Sweat pours from her brown skin. She wipes it away with her silk scarf and the beads of perspiration form immediately as soon as she wipes it away. She smells the tropical, moist, dirty fragrance of the jungle. She hears the chirping and the whirring and the silence. She closes her eyes for a long time. While she closes them, the scenery changes. The pungency of the jungle softens to the smell of familiar flowers and an artificial scent: the scent of ladies' perfume. The sound of the birds and the bugs relaxes into the sound of flutes, then horns, and then an entire band. At first she just stands there, with her eyes closed, breathing in the perfume and swaying to the swing of the band. When she opens her eyes, she is somewhere outside of New York, at a party, outdoors, on a wide veranda. The people are like long, tapering candles, a swarm of tuxedos and bias-cut silks. There are Japanese lanterns up in the trees, and a rolling lawn leading down to the water. Everything is lit, and fluttering, and painfully pretty. She sees people from her life dancing past her as she spins around on the dance floor, escorted by an invisible partner. She sees her father, dancing with Eleanor Roosevelt. The President is there, he's leading the band, and G.P. is having a smoke by the water. The feeling of the party is ominous and beautiful, decadent and lost.

We went into hiding. We had already made our decision, but because it was impossible for us to discuss it and we needed time to get ready, we said we were hiding, but really we were getting ready. We were getting ready to go.

We slept during the day in the darkest part of the jungle, and at night we prepared the Electra. By now she had been ravaged by the elements, although she was still beautiful, in a ravaged way. Her skin was rusted and her seams were loose, we had looted her and vandalized her to decorate our houses, her windshield was broken. But she was our last hope, and we lavished our attention on her in those last hours. Noonan said he loved her because she reminded him of me.

He unrolled the charts and reset the chronometer. He found his glasses, which he had long since forgotten about. They had fallen into one of the water tanks. She filled up coconuts with water and plugged them with leaves. She cleaned off the dashboard. They checked the fuel. They had a little left. They hadn't let themselves think about it, but now it seemed to them as precious as blood. They patched up the windshield. They mended the landing gear.

They don't talk about it anymore. It's understood that there's something in the air, something coming to take away their happiness, a shark circling in the sky. They know they have very little time, that the plane must have spotted the Electra, and possibly even them, and will be coming to get them soon.

In the hammock she lies with her head on his chest. He puts his arm around her. He says it's a good thing a plane's finally come for them. It's about time someone noticed they were missing. They are silent in the heat of the day. Sometimes he gets up to look through a hole in his shack at the sky. In the beginning, he used to get up to keep the fire going, but it's been a long time since they made an effort to be seen, and now they keep the fire out.

She sleeps soundly but not deeply, with her head on his chest, and he wakes her up with his tears.

We still went at night for a swim in the lagoon. We behaved as usual, and for a while we both continued to find happiness on the raft. We'd make love on the raft and our love would seem more intense, as if it were taking place on a magic carpet drifting over the ocean. We'd lie next to each other, naked, under the milky night sky, until somebody turned off the moon. But now we had no energy, no strength for love. It happened suddenly, without our realizing it. Our bodies couldn't pretend. They wanted nothing to do with leaving. Sometimes we were able to give each other pleasure, but it was painful. We did it anyway.

The wind has died down, and above the lagoon there's the otherworldly light that precedes dawn. A few birds are wailing their broken songs. As they wail, the sun breaks through the clouds, criminal, and slices like a knife across the water.

Fear revives them. He tells her to get her belongings — she has hardly any, just her logbook, her scarf, a hat — and she does. They had thought of taking the life raft from the plane and setting out. There seemed to be nothing to lose. But there were the sharks and the heat, and the realization that it would be harder to die than to go on living. Once before, they had chosen death, but had nevertheless continued to live. Now, without speaking, they both head toward the Electra.

The navigator feels so alone at the thought of losing her. The pleasure he takes in her, in being with her, is the only pleasure he knows anymore. He can't speak to her as they walk. He tries to take in the magnitude of their condition, but he can't. Nothing matters but the possibility of losing her. He realizes that without doing anything he has fallen in love, beyond love, out of love into life. It was on that walk, on the way to the Electra, that he let himself feel the full sadness of what he had never had before.

In the jungle, he looks at her. He can't stop looking at her, he sees her when his eyes are shut. He breathes her in, along with the smell of the jungle, his eyes shut, the jungle light electric blue behind his lids, the salty smell of her skin and her hair, he takes it in. In the jungle, in the dirty heat, he kisses her, and she kisses him, and they lie down together. They take each other on the floor of the jungle, and they know now that there is no difference between being rescued and being captured.

Part Three

. . . heaven did not seem to be my home; and I broke my heart with weeping to come back to earth; and the angels were so angry that they flung me out.

— EMILY BRONTË, *Wuthering Heights*

Twelve

In the Electra the light is blue. There's a smell of gasoline. The heat is heavy, there are no windows that open, so I leave the hatch up, but still the air is stifling.

I think maybe that he never said it, but that I only heard him say it, in silence. We were looking at each other, very hard, and I heard him say it without speaking and I said it too. His words entered my heart soundless, directly.

There is a time known as the between. The between voyager travels through uncharted territory, navigating dangers, attempting passage into the next life. There are times in life, after a death of some kind, when we are open to the slightest shifts, when our powers are acute, when we can change the future. *The between voyager temporarily possesses an immensely heightened intelli-*

*gence, extraordinary powers of concen-
tration, special abilities of clairvoyance
and teleportation, flexibility to become
whatever can be imagined, and the
openness to be radically transformed by
a thought or a vision or an instruction.*

More people should know this. We
should be taught this. This time never
announces itself, never tells us it is
here, or coming. But there are signs,
and ways of preparing. Life is the prepa-
ration. I had been risking my life without living it before, so I wasn't fully
prepared when my time came. But I had
a navigator. And so when my time came
again, a second time, I was prepared.

Planes used to be vehicles for dreaming. They were strong and curva-
ceous, manly and womanly at the same
time, simple, almost old-fashioned mechanical toys and vessels carrying the
future. As soon as you saw a plane, you
started dreaming. It was a thrill just to
catch a glimpse of one. In Los Angeles,
on hot nights, we used to drive out to
the airfield and watch the military pilots
practicing. Just landing and taking off.
We did it to get away from the heat, and

to dream even when we couldn't sleep. Large parts of the world were without airplanes. Back then, and it's not that long ago, most people in the world had never seen a plane, let alone been up in one.

Planes were not like ocean liners. They were not sprawling, they were intimate. They were not like towns with all the amenities of towns, they were like cars, or covered wagons. I think it was this, the intimacy of planes, the isolation, the privacy, the antisocial nature of flying a plane, this appealed to me. Everything that made ocean liner travel appealing ceased to exist in a plane. It was uncomfortable, you couldn't eat well, you couldn't dance or read a book. This was before many people started using planes for travel. Planes were mostly for mail, or for stunts. Many people still thought that airplanes were not for real people. That they were somehow ridiculous.

Takeoffs were not like ship departures. They were riveting, unpredictable, dangerous. There was not yet a ritual way of taking off in a plane, and each ascent was fraught with its own adventures. People have always departed, by land or sea, but to leave by air is still new, it is still a cause for wonder. Now, maybe by now, that's not true anymore. But at the time I'm describing, to leave in an airplane is as magical as taking off on a spaceship. It's a resurrection.

The Electra looked beautiful. She sat on the reef flat, enormous, expectant, waiting to take us away. But she didn't seem to want to go any more than we did. When it was time to go I climbed into the cockpit, and Noonan sat next to me, in the cockpit. He didn't go in back into the navigator's cabin because his instruments were mostly lost or broken and we needed to be closer to each other. Before he climbed in he checked everything one last time. He made sure that there were no birds trafficking our makeshift runway. Then he shut the hatch behind him. I tied on my scarf. I put on my goggles. Then I waved one last wave to the island, a cheerful wave, but the kind that always made everyone weep, with excitement and with the sadness of saying goodbye.

Then, very slowly, as if it were remembering how with all its might, the Electra lifted herself into the air. For a long time her distinctive shape could be seen rising toward the clouds. Many animals congregated on the beach and looked on, their heads lifting to follow the mysterious angel. And I thought I could see G.P. standing off to the side, the outline of the jungle juxtaposed archly behind him, his tie fluttering in the wind.

It was when we lifted above the first clouds, when the earth disappeared below us and the sky seemed to take up more space than the sea or the land, that I cried. I cried without letting Noonan see, because we were leaving together and there really wasn't anything to cry about. I tried to cry without letting him know and then I couldn't anymore and I just cried. He was silent and dark, sitting with his charts on his lap. I could feel that he was trembling. He was holding his glasses in his hand, and the glasses, they were trembling. He was overcome. I couldn't bear to look. I stared straight ahead, like before, so long ago, that night, our last night in the sky. I knew he was thinking the same thing.

There was the mindless roar of the engine, the quivering of the fuel gauge, the hot white sunlight reflecting off the windshield, but there was no more bamboo fishing pole, there was no need for that. Above all there was the sky. The widest, the most serene, the Pacific sky, as empty as a mind at peace. Sometimes it stretched out before us with the clarity of a single thought. There seemed to be nothing between us and our flight.

Very late at night, during the flight across the Pacific sky, they had a talk. She was tired, the moon was dim, Noonan was quiet. He was resting with his eyes closed. Then he started talking. He said he'd once known a fellow who'd set himself on fire. He was a sailor. They were sailors together. He'd been shipwrecked, alone, for ten days on a raft in the Indian Ocean, but had managed to survive. He'd eaten the money in his pockets and killed a seagull. He'd finally drifted toward land. That was years before. When Noonan knew him, he was a gambler. They gambled together. One night, in port, they were in the south of France, they were at a casino, a first-class casino, playing roulette. And all of a sudden the sailor excused himself, put out his cigarette, walked out of the casino, and shot himself in the head. But he didn't die. He went on living. The bullet lodged somewhere in his skull, but it didn't kill him. A few years later, after more seafaring, he set himself on fire.

The story was incredible to her, and for a moment it seemed as if everyone's story was fictional, as if all that was real were the bystanders, the people who told and retold the stories, not the characters themselves.

Later, she heard music. Not the music of Noonan's harmonica, but a celestial music, the music of the night. It was a sarabande. There was a gentle trade wind blowing across the emptiness, and it carried the music on its back and spread it like stardust over the ocean. She heard it clearly, vividly — it was written on the wind with the elliptical clarity of a telegram. It was playing very slowly, deliberately, each note dropping evenly, inevitably, after the one before. And she thought about the man setting himself on fire, to music, the music she was hearing. It seemed so morbid and melodramatic a thing to be thinking. But then she thought of her own life, just for a moment, and she thought that it could be seen that way too, operatic, overblown. But it didn't feel that way to her. It felt simple, and now, perfectly natural, as if it were an everyday river about to open onto a new sea.

The way of life is wonderful, she remembered. It is by abandonment.

Around her, the stars slept, not troubled or touched by the music. She felt a strong love for the night, and at the same time she realized that if her happiness were taken away from her, even Noonan, she would still be whole, with the same capacity for easy enjoyment from the world. She would not grieve. She had already done that. But she wished she could make everyone else feel how she felt, wished she could be sure that without her, he would still feel the perpetual revelations she felt. Then she would be happy. It was this feeling, and only this, that made her sad. That she might be leaving him with an unhappiness that he would not know how to cure. It was while she was thinking this that he opened his eyes and looked at her. His face was heavy.

Then he said, What are we having for dinner tonight?

Coconut, she said.

She doesn't know how long it was after they left the island that they ran out of fuel, found themselves lost once again over the Pacific Ocean. It happened in the morning. The heat was terrible. Everything happened as it had happened before: the plane stalled, then sputtered, then seemed to stop. She was frightened for a moment but then her sense of humor returned, and she guessed that somewhere, someone might be thinking she was a heroine.

When she woke from the lucid dream that carried her three thousand feet down, in a tumbling parade of images from the farthest reaches of her memory, her first impression was that she had died a violent death and gone directly to hell.

* * *

But this time she wasn't afraid. She knew that when she opened her eyes she would find a new island, more beautiful than the last, with the palm trees taller and more elegant, the beach wider and softer, the surf more accepting, calm.

It was true. Their brains intoxicated with the familiar smell of the sea, their bodies weak with hunger and exhaustion, they crawled out of the wreckage and looked around. It was just what she had expected. The wind was gentle. The air smelled like gardenias. The Electra had had a bad fall, but she was still standing. Her wings gleamed in the sunlight and cast long, graceful shadows, as if they were resting on the sand. Noonan walked down to the water and waded in up to his knees. She thought that with his long dark hair, his brown skin, and his long, brown limbs, he looked like a horse, naturally regal, looking out over the water.

I've told my story. I've written it in my pilot's log. I've read it to Noonan, who likes it very much. But he says that if

anyone ever read it, they wouldn't believe it. They'd say that it was a fantasy.

I'd say to them, If it is, then what have
I been doing all these years?

But sometimes I ask myself just that.
And then I feel the cold, ethereal
strangeness of existence.

One day, years later, when they were
relaxing in their hammocks on a hot
afternoon, he brought up the subject of
their flight around the world.

It seemed a distant memory. He
apologized to her for what had happened. Please don't worry about it, she
said. It was my fault too. Anyway, she
smiled, I forgive you for it. Thank you,
he said, and in his voice she heard
something. It was the sound of the
Electra. Then he said, What a day. It
was hot, but she'd known worse. He
said maybe later they'd go for a swim
in the lagoon. Then they were silent for
a long time. And then she broke down.
Broke down in tears, tears of joy, mysterious tears, and said, Yes, this must
be real, I believe in this life. I believe
that it continues.

Acknowledgments

This story is a work of fiction. It was inspired by the life and disappearance of Amelia Earhart; however, the portraits of the characters who appear in it are fictional, as are many of the events described.

Several books were important to me during my research. *Amelia Earhart: A Biography* by Doris L. Rich was especially useful for factual information. Earhart's own *Last Flight* provided a description of her final journey, and the lines in italics on page 60 are from her book. The lines in italics on page 17 are from Charles Lindbergh's memoir, *The Spirit of St. Louis*. Richard Gillespie's article "The Mystery of Amelia Earhart" was also useful for factual information. The lines in italics on pages 173–174 are from Robert A. F. Thurman's commentary in his translation of *The Tibetan*

Book of the Dead.

Many friends read versions of this book in manuscript form, and I am grateful to all of them for their insights and encouragement. In particular, special thanks to James Wood, Andrew Solomon, Seth and Joanna Hendon, and Melissa Marks. For their faith in this book and their efforts on its behalf, I would like to thank Ann Close, Nelly Bly, Joy Harris, Robin Robertson, and Sonny Mehta. I'd also like to thank my family for their support, especially Evelyn Driesen and Martha Mendelsohn.

And finally, most of all, thank you to my mother and father, with gratitude and love.

The employees of Thorndike Press hope you have enjoyed this Large Print book. All our Large Print titles are designed for easy reading, and all our books are made to last. Other Thorndike Large Print books are available at your library, through selected bookstores, or directly from us.

For information about titles, please call:

(800) 223-2336

To share your comments, please write:

Publisher
Thorndike Press
P.O. Box 159
Thorndike, Maine 04986